Ina E. Wood Van Norman

Minnewaska - A Legend of Lake Mohonk

Sequel to Longfellow's Hiawatha - And Other Lyrical Poems

Ina E. Wood Van Norman

Minnewaska - A Legend of Lake Mohonk
Sequel to Longfellow's Hiawatha - And Other Lyrical Poems

ISBN/EAN: 9783744786720

Printed in Europe, USA, Canada, Australia, Japan

Cover: Foto ©Andreas Hilbeck / pixelio.de

More available books at **www.hansebooks.com**

MINNEWASKA

A Legend of Lake Mohonk

SEQUEL TO

LONGFELLOW'S HIAWATHA

AND OTHER LYRICAL POEMS

——— ——

BY

INA E. WOOD VAN NORMAN

PUBLISHED BY
DONOHUE & HENNEBERRY
CHICAGO, ILL.

ILLUSTRATED BY J. T. TASKER.
ENGRAVINGS BY MINNEAPOLIS ENGRAVING CO.

CONTENTS.

PREFACE.

In presenting this collection of poems, songs, etc., to my friends to whom this volume is dedicated, it has been my only thought that among them there might be found something that may be pleasing or otherwise entertaining. If so, I shall feel amply recompensed for my endeavors; although I feel assured that there will be found many imperfections, and much occasion for adverse criticism, yet I beg a lenient judgment, and in making this, my humble contribution to the Poetic art, I feel I owe an apology for the seeming encroachment on the grounds which our distinguished poet has so thoroughly covered in his beautiful poem Hiawatha; and would but say, as the only extenuating excuse, that the key to the solution will be found in the following lines, quoted from Minnewaska:

> For the tent is lone and the wigwam drear
> When the smiles of youth can give no cheer;
> And murmuring voices from far off space
> Echoed the words through silent space.

'Tis even so with poetry and other forms of literature. There seems ever room for new thoughts, new modes of expression, which, like an infant's advent in an already numerous family, there is generally to be found room for just one more. Thus it is to be hoped that art, word painting and literature may never grow old, but ever continue to refine, elevate and ennoble our minds, until we have attained that perfection to which we all aspire.

Your friend,

Mrs. Lucien P. Van Norman.

INTRODUCTORY NOTES

TO MINNEWASKA.

Facts Gleaned from Indian Myths and Legends.

Minnewaska, or the Legend of Lake Mohonk, is partially founded upon the Indian supposition or tradition of the creation of the earth by one of their chief gods, whom they designated Unk-te-hee, the god of earth and water; and also upon their belief of the enmity existing between him-self and Wakin-yan-tanka, the god of thunder, a sardonic spirit, whom they imagine comes in the midst of the storm to do battle with Unk-te-hee, the spirit of earth and water. The Dakotas be-lieve that thunder is produced by the flapping of the wings of a huge bird which they call Wakin-yan, the thunder bird, and it is said near the source of the Minnesota River is a place called Thunder-tracks, where the foot-prints of a thunder bird can be found twenty-five miles apart. Tradi-tions say there are many thunder birds. Wakin-yan-tanka, or Big Thunder, having his dwelling place on a lofty mountain in the far West, and having a bitter hatred toward Unk-te-hee (the god of waters), often shoots his fiery arrows at him, hitting the earth, trees, rocks, and some-times man. Traditions also say that great Unk-te-

7

hee and the great thunder bird Wakin-yan-tanka, had a terrible battle in the center of the earth to determine which should be the ruler of the world. (See Rigs' Tah-koo, and Mrs. Eastman's Dakota.) Oonk-tay-he is the pronunciation of the word Unk-te-hee. There are many Unk-te-hees, children of the great Unk-te-hee, the creator of the earth and man, and who formerly dwelt in a vast cavern, the place around about being called Ka-tha-ga, the cavern itself supposedly being situated beneath the Falls of St. Anthony, Minnesota. 'Tis said the great Unk-te-hee sometimes reveals himself, and from him proceed invisible influences. (See Gordon's "Winona").

There are many of the wild tribes who believe in a great creative power and a great destructive power, continually striving together and finding form in the Unk-te-hees, and the thunder birds, or Wakin-yans, who are perpetually at war, one with the other. It is also said that after Unk-te-hee had finished the earth, beasts, birds, and fishes and all that dwelt therein, he bade man spring forth from a huge hollow mountain and from among them he chose him a band, naming them after himself Unk-te-hees, and claiming them as his sons he made them lords over the beasts, birds, and fishes and all that lived on the earth or swam in the waters, and instructed them to obey his commands as follows: Ye shall honor Unk-te-hee and hate Wakin-yan the god of thunder; ye shall laugh at his darts, and, in need ye shall pray to the great god of waters; ye shall dwell together in peace; ye shall dwell as a strong band of brothers, ye are men whom I choose for my own; ye are

those whom I choose from all others; ye shall wor-
ship the earth and the sun, for they are your father
and mother, and forget not the Invisible Power,
the Invisible great Taku-Wakan, who pervades
all the earth and the air, who invisibly dwells in
all matter; fear not the darts of a foe, for the warrior's brave soul is immortal; hold as sacred the
innocent babe; slay not the wife or the mother;
when a stranger arrives at the tee, be he friend,
be he foe, give him succor; let your food and your
bounty be free; lend a robe as you would to a
brother; hold as sacred thy word, and, in need, ye
shall sacrifice self for another; yes, forfeit thy life
for a brother. Now, into thy keeping I give the
magical pouch of the spirits, the magical art, and
the bone, and my voice ye shall harken and heed
it. Thus long shall ye live in the land, and the
spirit of earth and of water, shall come to your aid
at command, with invisible power of magic. And
at last, when your journeys are done, and ye reach
the fair land of Po-ne-ma, ye shall walk as a bright
shining star, in the land of eternal hereafter—Imi-
tation H. L. Gordon's beautiful poem Winona.

* * *

Minnewaska and Lake Mohonk are two lovely
little lakes—gems in themselves of all that is
beautiful, romantic and picturesque in nature—
situated as they are in close proximity to each
other, on one of the higher portions of the Shaw
angunk Mountains and surrounded on all sides by
their wild and rocky scenery, wooded heights,
and sloping ravines, they form a picture once seen
never to be forgotten. Strange and weird in the

evening shadows, Lake Mohonk lies calm and
still with unruffled bosom, placidly reflecting the
gigantic cliffs, bowlders and over-hanging growth
of luxuriant verdure, mid the clear green of its
shining waters; deep, dark and mysterious, its
waters gleam like a sparkling jewel 'neath its rugged setting of towering walls, massive bowlders
and projecting rocks that hem it in, with an almost
impenetrable wall of strength and grandeur. Many
and strange were the legends told in the past time,
of the wonderful formation of so large a body of
water, springing apparently from the bowels of the
earth to nearly the topmost part of a mountain
over seventeen hundred feet above the level of the
Hudson. Many years ago this place was known as
the Giant's basin, and there is now an almost forgotten tradition that the great cavern-like walls
were hewn out by the giant strength of an Indian
god, and the waters, formed by the same miracu-
lous power welled up from the deep and hidden
recesses of the earth, forming a singular and almost ideal beauty of what is now known as Lake
Mohonk. There is apparently no inlet or outlet
to this lake, though many are of the opinion there
is a subterranean connection between it and Lake
Minnewaska, the clear and beautiful lake adjoin-
ing, whose bright and shining waters flow in the
most charming and graceful way over the precipi- .
tous rocks in cascade upon cascade, over the
terrace-like walls, till with one mighty leap it
plunges down the precipitous sides of the mountain to the valley below, where for a distance of
several miles, the shining fall of water can be seen,
gleaming like a stream of molten silver 'neath the

golden rays of the noon-day sun. Near by stand
the vine and moss-clad walls of Castle Rock, bold
and conspicuous amid its wild and weird surround-
ings, of cliff and bowlder, rocky caverns and
deep fissures, that sink away apparently to the
very center of the earth. Here among the rocky
wildness and lonely silence, one might easily
imagine some supernatural power had formed and
fashioned for itself this strange and massive struct-
ure. Hewn from the solid rocks, into the veritable
semblance of the embrasured, parapeted and
domed castle of the ancient times, it stands a fitting
dwelling place for e'en the gods of old, and forming one of the now justly celebrated attractions
of the Shawangunk Mountains.

The following are a few extracts taken from
newspaper notices of prominent people and others
who have visited this beautiful and altogether
charming locality.

EXTRACTS FROM NEWSPAPER NOTICES.

REV. A. D. MAYO, IN SUNDAY TELEGRAM:

"Then two weeks at Sky Top and Lake Mohonk, one of those rare places where the creative
power seems to have rehearsed for every form
of grandeur and gentleness; an Alpine lake on
top of a mountain 1,200 feet above the valley,
the mountain itself a gigantic monument of rock
scenery wrought into every form of wildness
and grace, and from any point on the summit
cliffs an outlook over two perfect valleys, with

fifty miles of the western horizon crowded with
glorious mountain ranges, amid whose mysterious
realms the sinking sun and the morning mist
work such magic as only poetry exalted to wor-
ship can fitly rehearse."

NEW YORK EVENING POST:

"Up, up we climbed above the monarchs of
the forest, up to where the air is rarefied, up to
the height of a thousand feet or more; when, lo!
a vision of enchantment is before us. O, divers
after beauty! here is the pearl of it—the crystal,
hill-locked Mohonk Lake. We wish we could
describe it to you as it looked that bright July
day, sparkling in the sunlight, as it always looks,
for no strife of the elements, however fierce,
ruffles or disturbs its placidity. The storm king
cannot even jog its rock-bound cradle."

REV. DR. LYMAN ABBOTT, IN CHRISTIAN WEEKLY:

"I have never seen such a variety of beauties
crowded into so small a compass—lake, mountain,
rock and wide extended plain; here a succession
of cabinet pictures of most exquisite finish, there
a panorama measured by a score of miles. The
lake is a gem, exquisite in itself and exquisite in
its setting. Its clear water is an emerald green.
In one little cove, where for the past half hour
my boat has been lying, the rocks are turned to
emerald by the reflection of the water. All
around, the rocky sides rise in precipitous cliffs,
or in masses of huge stones tumbled together in
sublime confusion. Pine Bluff, which shades me
from the setting sun as I write, rises fully fifty
feet—literally a perpendicular wall—from the

water's edge. The two sentinels which guard the gateway to this little lake are, the one three hundred feet, the other two hundred; the former nearly perpendicular, the other quite so. If I leave the lake and ascend either of these cliffs, the panoramic scene is one which defies alike the pen or pencil. The view from the Catskills is wider in range, but here we are on the edge of a knife blade, and either side commands a prospect equally extended. In this respect I remember no mountain peak that compares with it, not even Mt. Holyoke, which it somewhat resembles. * * * We clambered along the mountain side, now down through a deep chasm or cliff in the rock, whose walls tower one hundred feet above us, brushing our shoulders on either side; now across a similar chasm, looking down from our frail bridge in a cliff as deep beneath our feet; now peering into a cave, whose subterranean recesses I did not care to explore; now into another, where bubbled up a mountain spring of clear, cold water; now clambering down again by aid of laurel bushes which have grown to trees, whose trunks my two hands cannot clasp. while all the way is rich with moss and ferns and lichens, whose varying tints of green and brown make every step afford a new revelation."

IRENAEUS, IN NEW YORK OBSERVER:

"The little world in which the lake is embosomed has peculiar attractions, which the amateur geologist or intelligent visitor studies with increasing wonder as he goes up and down among these rocks and dells, and caves and dens of the earth, so that days and weeks are pleasantly spent in exploring the mysterious caverns, the Giant's Workshop and Eagle Cliff, and gazing upon the Old Man of the Mountains."

Rev. J. B. Wakely, D. D., in Newburg Journal:

"I think I never had larger ideas of beauty, grandeur and magnificence. * * * 'Tis difficult to paint a diamond, a sun, a rainbow; 'tis equally difficult to describe the indescribable. What a pencil I need, what canvas, what colors, to do justice to such a scene, and then I would need an angel's hand to guide the pencil."

Rev. Dr. Krotel, in the Lutheran:

"A few rods more and we began to descend the mountain, and in a few moments caught the first glimpse of Mohonk Lake, one of the most beautiful mountain lakes, and unquestionably one of the greatest surprises in the Atlantic States * * * You do not expect to find such a body of water up there. It would be difficult to find a spot more interesting and beautiful."

INDIAN VOCABULARY.

Han-ye-tu-wee—The night sun or moon.
An-pe-tu-wee—The day sun.
Eto, E-ho—Exclamations of delight.
Unk-te-hce—The god of water.
Mee-tah-win—My bride.
Wakin-yan-tanka—The god of thunder; big thunder.
Wakan-denda—The meteor, or sacred fire.
Wakan-wo-halpa—A sacred gift.
Enah—An exclamation of wonder, surprise or delight.
Gitche-man-ito—The great spirit, the giver of life.
Po-ne-mah—The hereafter.
Anne-me-kee—The thunder.
Ope-chee—The robin.
Chit-o-walk—The plover.
Ogema—Chieftain.
Man-ito—A god.
Wo-hon-o-win —A cry of lamentation, or woe is me.
Onaway—Awake.
Kah-no-te-deha—A mysterious spirit of the woods.
Owais-sa—The blue bird.
Nene-moo-sha—My sweetheart.
Wakan-dee—The lightning.
Jeebi—A spirit, or angel.

Wangee-ta-chan-ku—The milky way, or the pathway of spirits.

Mee-heen-yah—My husband.

Ta-toka—The mountain antelope.

Ta-hin-ca—The red deer.·

Tam-doka—The buck deer.

Ta-hin-ca-ska—The white mountain deer (sheep).

Oonk-to-mee—A spirit inhabiting fens and marshes, the ignis fatuus or jack-o-lantern.

Ka-tha-ga—Literally the place of waves and foam; and 'twas said between two and three centuries ago was situated under the "Falls of St. Anthony."

Dakota—Signifies an alliance or confederation; many separate Indian tribes united under this name, including the Mohawks, Delawares and other eastern tribes.

Tee-pee—A lodge or wigwam, often contracted to tee.

MINNEWASKA.

A Legend of Lake Mohonk.

Sequel to

Longfellow's Hiawatha.

Minne-ha-ha, laughing water,
Fair Dakota's lovely daughter,
I have wandered far to find thee,
I have left fair scenes behind me,
Many moons t'ward the eastward,
From the heights of the Shawangunk,
From the depths of caverns lonesome,
Through the Mohawk's sunny vale,
Through the wild-wood's tangled trail,
O'er the meadows, hills and valleys,
O'er the waving green prairies,
Have I wandered, Minne-ha-ha,
Fair Dakota's lovely daughter.
I have viewed thy royal splendor,
Sublime thy beauty and thy grandeur,

With thy shimmering robes around thee,
Laughing water, have I found thee:
Dancing, where the sunbeams play,
Mystic, 'neath the moonbeam's ray,
Sparkling, circling, plunging downward,
Whirling, floating, gliding onward,
Making music with thy laughter—
Gladsome, winsome, Minne-ha-ha.
Crowned with beauty, have I found thee,
Pale-faced race with honors crowned thee,
Fairest of the laughing waters—
Fair and winsome, Minne-ha-ha.
I am called U-a-no-ma, wandering spirit of the
    night,
U-a-no-ma, the great wanderer, daughter of the
    pale moonlight.
Oft have I sat, where thy tall trees sway,
Close by thy side, where the night shades play,
When the starlight shines, and the gentle breeze
Floats through the boughs of thy bending trees;
Wrapt in the spell of the witching scenes,
Heard thy voice blend with my waking dreams;
And thy echoing music, like a charmful spell,

MINNE-HA-HA FALLS, MINN.

On the night winds float through thy shadowy
   dell.
But when storm clouds, drifting o'er the moon,
Shroud thee deep in mist and gloom,
Then doth thy spirit, 'neath the spell of the hour,
Bow in the sadness of memory's power:
And I hear thee sigh, like a soul in pain,
Sigh and weep, like the falling rain:
Wohon-o-win! wohon-o-win! oh, my daughter,
My fair, my loved, my Minnewaska.
And the tall trees echo thy tender sigh,
Sway and moan, as the winds sweep by
And pain and sadness doth rend thy heart,
When storms are fierce and clouds are dark.
And I hear thee sigh, like a soul in pain,
Sigh and weep, like the falling rain:
Wohon-o-win! wohon-o-win! oh, my daughter,
My loved, my lost, my Minnewaska.
In silence I've sat, 'neath enchantment's power,
Close by thy side at midnight's hour,
And a spirit's voice, from a far off sphere,
Came floating like music, my soul could hear,
And whispered a secret, a strange wild tale,

And I knew why you wept when the night winds
    wail.
And the spirit's voice bade me wandering go,
Sit close by thy side where thy waters flow,
And tell thee a tale that will ease thy heart,
When storms are fierce and clouds are dark;
And thy spirit shall wake from an evil spell,
And leap for joy at U-a-no-ma's tale.

TALE OF U-A-NO-MA.

In the days of the Dacotahs,
Fair, bright days of the Dacotahs,
In the lands that are afar off,
Where oft the winds blow from the north;
Downward from the pale moonlight,
Fell a gleaming star at night.
Close by the side of a wild-wood tent,
Was the shining course of the meteor bent,
On the cold white earth, all snowy bound,
Was the form of a little infant found.
Where the meteor left its shining trail,
Now came the infant's piteous wail.
Now stept a spirit out from night,

Kah-no-te-daha, the forest sprite.

Softly she tread, with a footfall light,

Out neath the gloom of the pale moonlight,

And clasped the child in her strong right arm,

As she crossed to the tent with a quickening
 bound;

Light was her step, and she made no sound,

As swiftly she sped o'er the frozen ground.

Aside she swept the curtained door,

Stept lightly o'er the matted floor,

Bent o'er the form of a woman fair,

With laughing eyes and shining hair.

At her feet she laid the infant babe,

And in tones that were softly sweet and grave,

Spoke in a voice with a far off sound,

Like the whispering winds, as they murmured
 'round.

Minne-ha-ha! laughing water,

Fair Dacotah's lovely daughter,

From the midnight's pale, starry height,

From wakan-denda, the meteor light,

Mid the sacred rays of the meteor star,

Was borne this babe, from realms afar.

Look thou, then, on the infant fair,
With eyes like thine, and shining hair;
Fair as the moon when it gleams at night,
Bright as the sun when it sheds its light;
Beauty and grace in face and form,
To thee was the child of the midnight born.
We have named her Minnewaska,
Thy fair daughter, Minnewaska;
For the tent is lone, and the wigwam drear,
When the smiles of youth can give no cheer;
And murmuring voices from far off space,
Echoed the words through the silent place;
And the spirit leaned o'er the babe in prayer,
Then swiftly fled through the midnight air.
Thus was born to Minne-ha-ha,
At midnight's hour, fair Minnewaska;
And thou cherished her, and loved her,
Taught the child to call thee mother,
Taught the young life, in useful art,
Of home and duty, to share a part;
Taught the young hands, with fanciful grace,
The mantle's broider'd design to trace,
And the rainbow colors, with blended hue,

Taught the young feet through the wilds to roam,
Bearing the fruit of the harvest home;
And the lily, and rose, and mossy vine,
Then taught the maiden in wreaths to twine,
To deck the feast, and the campfire's dance,
When home came the warriors with spear and lance.

Were strewn o'er garments that shone like dew;
And the fairy lace the weaver wove,
Were like fleecy clouds the breezes blowed.
Taught the young feet through the wilds to roam,
Bearing the fruits of the harvest home;
And the lily, and rose, and mossy vine,
Thou taught the maiden in wreaths to twine,
To deck the feast, and the camp-fire's dance,
When home came the warriors with spear and
  lance:
Taught the young voice, and the forest rang
Like the night bird's song, when the maiden sang.
Through the mazy dance, like a rhythmic tide,
Taught the young form to sway and glide;
And the rippling laugh of her own sweet voice,
Taught the maiden's heart how to rejoice.
Thus thou cherished her and taught her,
Loved and cherished thy fair daughter.
But the years of her childhood quickly fled,
And a fair young maiden reigned instead,
Tall and stately, like the lilies fair
She twined in the braids of her shining hair.
And the sounding music of her laughter

Echoed long, and followed after.

Lovely and pure as the sparkling water,

Was the fair young maiden, Minnewaska.

Yet alas! alas! oh, Minne-ha-ha!

Alas! alas! fair Minnewaska!

An evil Manito, on mischief bent,

At an evil hour passed by thy tent.

The Wakin-yan-tanka, the storm god disguised,

On thee and thine had fixed his eyes;

Jealous of thy watchful care

Bestowed upon thy child so fair,

Jealous of thy words and teachings,

O'er thee spread his evil wings;

Vowed his evil vows against thee,

To molest thee and destroy thee.

And thy heart grew sick to fainting,

With evil omen and foreboding;

Renewed thy ever watchful care

O'er thy sweet child, so young and fair:

But he laughed in loud derisions,

Taunting thee with spells and visions.

Once he leaped a space before thee,

And darkness of night loomed black before thee;

Twice he leaped, and a cloud descended—
Slowly downward it descended;
And thy daughter, lo! thy fair daughter,
In its fierce dark folds it caught her,
Wrapped its great black folds about her,
Whirling, swirling, up it bore her;
And the evil Man-ito, with mocking laughter,
Leaped up through space, and followed after.
Up and away from thy frenzied sight,
Through the storm and darkness of the night.
But at midnight's hour the spell was broken,
And thy fast sealed eyelids slowly opened;
A death white pallor o'erspread thy brow,
A strange wild dread had seized thee now,
And gazing with anguish and terror blent,
Thine eyes roamed round thy silent tent;
And thy changed voice shrieked in wild despair,
Echoed long on the midnight air,
Oh! my daughter, my fair sweet daughter,
Where art thou, where, oh, Minnewaska?
Only the night winds heard thy plaintive cry,
Only the night winds echoed thy sad reply.
Oh, my daughter, heed thy mother's prayer,

Answer me, my child, where art thou, where?
But the tent was silent, the wigwam lone:
In vain through the forest did thy footsteps roam,
And the wilds resound with thy lost child's name'
She came not back to thy tent again.
The days and months and years have flown,
But she came not back to thy forest home:
And pain and sadness o'erpressed thy heart,
When storms were fierce and clouds were dark,
And thou breathed a sigh like a soul in pain;
Sighed and wept like the falling rain.
Oh, my daughter, my wandering daughter,
Where art thou, where, my Minnewaska?
The days and months and years rolled by,
When fever and famine and want drew nigh,
Breathed o'er thee their blasting breath,
And thy form lay silent and still in death,
And thy spirit, freed from all toil and pain,
Sought the blest haunts of thy childhood's reign,
Still when the winds sweep o'er thy vale,
Doth thy spirit sigh, when the night winds wail,
Woho-no-win, woho-no-win, oh, my daughter,
Where art thou, where, oh Minnewaska?

But the evil Man-ito with spells and art,

Hath power no more to grieve thy heart;

To-night the gods of fate have spoken,

The evil spells round thee are broken.

Thou shalt know the fate of Minnewaska.

Listen, then, oh, Minne-ha-ha!

To the words of U-a-no-ma.

U-A-NO-MA'S TALE—CONTINUED.

In a vale far to the eastward,

By a lone camp-fire a chieftain stood;

A brave young warrior, whose tossing plume

Waved to and fro in the midnight gloom,

Dark was the night, and storms raged 'round him,

Sighed the winds through each swaying limb,

The fire light leaped and danced before him,

Lighting the face of the warrior grim:

As he stood like a statue carved from stone,

That shrouded his form in the valley lone.

With head erect and eyes agleam,

He gazed aloft at the wild night scene,

At the raging battles the skies portrayed,

Where the thunder roared and the lightnings
    played.

But a shudder ran through his tall, lithe form,
When a fierce dark cloud o'erhead was borne,
Whirling, swirling, onward it came,
Mid the rushing winds and falling rain.
Then a sudden hush and the storm had ceased,
Not a breath of wind through the valley breathed;
The night grew dense as the dark-winged cloud
Reeled 'round through space like a palling shroud.
A deafening roar, a thundering crash,
And through the heavens a bright light flashed,
Like a meteor ray through the dark of night,
Fell a gleaming star on the warrior's sight;
Like an arrow shot from the bended bow,
It sped through space to the earth below.
Long the warrior gazed through the vale afar,
Where blazed the light of the phantom star,
Then leaped a space with a swift, light bound,
He sped like a roe o'er the turfted ground;
On through the shadows and gloom of night,
He strode through the vale t'ward the mystic
    light,
As it swayed like a phantom's fitful gleam,
Like the Oonk-to-mee swayed and beckoned him.

Like a meteor ray through the dark of night,
Fell a gleaming star on the warrior's sight;
Like an arrow shot from the bended bow,
It sped through space to the earth below.

On o'er the meadows and through wilds afar,

He followed the trail of the shining star;

On through the darkness and storms of night,

He followed the rays of the mystic light.

Down through the depths of a rocky dell,

Where evil spirits and wizards dwell;

A sudden flash and the phantom light

Faded in silence and gloom of night.

A rift of clouds and the silvery moon

Shone through the shades of the midnight gloom;

Deep in the heart of the rocky dell

The shimmering light of the pale moon fell,

O'er the still white form of a maiden fair,

With lilies twined in her streaming hair;

In 'broidered mantle all royal rayed,

Laid the sleeping form of an Indian maid.

Fair as a statue carved from stone,

She lay where the rays of the moonlight shone;

And the warrior strode with a swift, light tread,

And leaned o'er her form on the moss-grown bed.

Aside he swept her flowing hair,

Gazed long on her features pale and fair,

Long and silent as in a dream,

O'er the maiden's form the warrior leaned;
Then raised his eyes to the star-lit dome,
Whispered in low, soft undertone,
Thou art fair as am-pe-tu-wee, that gives us light,
Fair as han-ye-tu-wee that shines at night.
Jeebi or maid, from what far off sphere,
From what far off land hast wandered here?
From the far off shores of the po-ne-mah,
Hast wandered from the great hereafter?
Onaway, he whispered softly,
Hast thy fair spirit come to haunt me?
Or hast fell from the wings of wakin-yan-tanka—
The wings of the thunder god, wakin-yan-tanka,
Down from anne-me-kee, the thunder of night,
Led by the oonk-to-mee's pale, phantom light?
Hath drifted down through the storm and gloom,
To the magic vale of fate and doom?
Onaway! my heart speaks to thee,
Sings with joy when thou art near me
Onaway! from thy death-like sleep
I bid thee 'wake, arise, and speak!
But the maiden's lips gave forth no sound,
As silent she lay on the moss-grown mound.

Wohon-o-win! the evil Manito of this wizard dell
Hath cast o'er thee enchantment's spell,
Bound thy fair form 'neath an evil power,
'Neath the magic spell of the midnight hour,
By all the powers opposed to fate,
Fair maid, I bid thee 'rise, awake!
And with clap of hand and springing bound,
The warrior leaped over the turfted ground,
And spoke in tones of stern command,
As he waved o'er her form his swaying hand;
By all the powers opposed to fate,
Fair maid, I bid thee 'rise, awake!
Still the maiden lay in a silent trance,
Nor heeded the warrior's strange, wild glance,
Nor heeded his wail of wild despair,
As it echoed long on the midnight air.
A sudden flash, a dazzling light
Shone through the shadows and gloom of night,
A thundering crash, a rushing sound,
A dark form swayed o'er the trembling ground;
And wakin-yan-tanka, with dark wings spread,
Now leaned over the maid on her moss-grown
    bed:

Leaned o'er her couch with a fiendish glare,
As his mocking laugh rent the midnight air.
With winged arms, like a threatening cloud,
He leaned o'er her bed like a palling shroud:
With winged arms and swaying hand,
He waved o'er her form his magic wand;
Fiercer and fiercer his wild eyes gleamed,
Closer and closer his dark form leaned;
A fearful roar, a muttering tone,
And his voice rang far through the valley lone:
By all the powers of wind and storm,
By all the elements and power I own,
By my lightning's fire and my thunder's roar,
By my wings of air on which I soar,
By all the storm fiends, alive or dead,
By my magic rule this maid I'll wed.
Bride of the midnight's stormy skies,
By all my powers, awake! arise!
A clash of wings, a deafening roar,
Rolled round through space and echoed o er,
A mocking laugh Wakin-yan-tanka breathed,
A cloud of mist o'er the maiden wreathed,
A piercing shriek on the night air fell.

And the maid awoke from her magic spell.

A mocking laugh on the winds was borne,

An answering shout through the mist and storm,

And the warrior chief with hurrying bound,

Leaped through the shades and shadows round;

Then paused a space, with eyes ablaze

At Wakin-yan-tanka the warrior gazed,

Long and steadily, his towering form

Swayed like a reed 'neath a coming storm;

Slowly and steadily, with eyes that gleamed,

T'ward Wakin-yan-tanka the warrior leaned,

Then spoke, and his voice gave a hollow sound,

Like the deep flow of waters through caverns
    round.

Hark thee, Wakin-yan-tanka, I know thee well,

I fear not thee or thy magic spell,

Thy thundering bolts or thy storm-winged clouds,

Thy flashing lights or thy palling shrouds;

Ho! thou spirit, coward at soul,

Quakes 'neath the power of Unk-te-hee's control.

Unk-te-hee, the god of the rocks and the water;

Unk-te-hee, who dwells in the midst of earth
    matter;

Who dwells in the stone, the mountain and river,

E-ho! the avenger of wrong, makes thy coward
　　soul quiver;

Mighty and strong, thou doth fear him forever.

Unk-te-hee, the god of the rocks and the water,

Laughs at thy darts, at thy black wings of
　　thunder.

The great warrior Mohonk, son of great Unk-
　　te-hee,

Laughs thee to scorn, his heart doth not fear thee.

And with springing bound and clap of hand,

The warrior spoke in stern command:

By all the powers of Unk-te-hee the great,

By all the powers opposed to fate,

By all the spirits of earth and air,

Unk-te-hee, hear thy warrior's prayer.

Unk-te-hee, great father, thou great god of water,

Endow me with magic, the magic of wonder,

Heed me, thy son, Unk-te-hee, thy warrior,

Commands of the strength o'er thy foe, the
　　destroyer,

The magical wand of the river and mountain,

The magical wand of the stream and the fountain;

Give wings to my feet that o'er mountain and
  river,
I may speed like the wind through the forest and
  heather;
Give thy magical darts, the bow and the quiver,
That thy enemy's blood may flow like the river;
Give strength to my aim when my arrow goes
  speeding
Swift through the mist, where the storm god is
  breathing;
Ho! at my feet may he lie stunned and bleeding.
A clap of hands, a springing bound,
And the warrior's shout re-echoed 'round;
A mocking laugh on the night air fell,
An answering shout rang through the dell,
A whirling mist and wild winds raged,
Bright lights, conflicting, a moment blazed,
A deafening roar, a bright light flashed,
A thundering bolt o'er the warrior crashed
A crouching form and the warrior leaned,
Through swaying shadows his fierce eyes
  gleamed;
A steady aim and his bended bow,

Gave forth a clang like a knell of woe.
A whizzing sound and his arrow sped,
Swift through the whirling mist it sped;
A clash of wings, a heaving sound,
A dark form reeled through the mist around,
A maddening roar, a sullen groan,
Wakin-yan-tanka lay stunned in the valley lone.
Enah, enah, e-ho, e-ho,
The warrior's shout rang o'er his foe;
With leap like a panther protecting its young,
O'er Wakin-yan-tanka the warrior sprung.
With gliding pace and a magic tread,
The warrior strode toward the moss-grown bed,
Where the maiden lay in a sudden swoon,
'Neath the gleaming light of the waning moon.
Long and silent the warrior leaned
O'er the maid, where the lights and shadows
    gleamed;
Then raised her form from her lowly bed,
With winged feet through the night he sped.
On through the depths of the rocky wilds,
On o'er bowlders and steep defiles,
On o'er caverns where cataracts roar,

The pale, white form of the maid he bore.

On o'er the brink, through the midnight gloom,

He sped from the vale of fate and doom,

And his wild shout echoed his loud enah!

As he sped away through the wilds afar.

An answering echo, a shuddering moan,

Quaked through the depths of the valley lone,

A shuddering sigh, Wakin-yan-tanka breathed,

A cloud of mist o'er the sleeper wreathed,

A clap of wings and his prostrate form

Reeled from earth, through the mist and storm.

A quaking shudder, a reeling bound,

His dark form swayed o'er the trembling ground,

A mocking laugh, an answering shout,

Amid the winds of the night rang out,

And Wakin-yan-tanka, with huge wings spread,

Whirled o'er the path where the warrior tread:

Up and away through the starry night,

He followed the warrior's hurried flight,

On o'er meadows and through meads afar,

He followed the trail through the wilds afar;

On o'er the mountain, the river and stream,

On through the forest and rocky ravine,

On through the shadows and shades of night,
He followed the warrior's hurried flight.
On mid the rushing and quaking storm,
The dark wing form of the fiend was borne;
On and mid roar and thundering crash,
His lightning darts o'er the warrior flashed;
On till the rays of the early morn
Streaked the night shades with a golden dawn;
On till An-pe-tu-wee came swiftly striding,
Swift o'er the storm god his footsteps came gliding,
On till An-pe-tu-wee, the sun god of great wonder,
Arose o'er the storm god, the great god of thun-
     der—
Arose in his beauty, his flashing eyes gleaming,
O'er Wakin-yan-tanka sent his fiery darts stream-
     ing,
On till his swift rays rent the storm clouds
     asunder—
Rent the dark clouds, pierced the great god of
     thunder.
Then like a phantom retreating from sight,
With low, muttering rumble he vanished from
     sight;

CASTLE ROCK, MOHONK LAKE, NEW YORK.

Far up the Shawangunk's steep mountain height
He bore the mazed I'ward the open light;
Far up the mount where his castle dome
'Neath the golden rays of the sunlight shone.

With low, mocking laughter and rumbling sound,

He reeled through space with a whirling bound;

Back through the shades and shadows afar,

His form grew dim as a fading star.

And the warrior's shout rang a loud enah!

As he sped away through the wilds afar;

On t'ward the east, t'ward the rising sun,

With every stride a league he sprung.

Far up a valley, the Mohawk vale,

The maid he bore through a sunny dale;

Far up the Shawangunk's steep mountain height

He bore the maid t'ward the open light.

Far up the mount, where his castle dome,

'Neath the golden rays of the sunlight shone,

And its shining walls glistened and gleamed,

Where the golden rays of the sunlight streamed,

And the waving vine swayed to and fro,

From the rocky dome to the base below.

Wild and weird, with hurried tread,

T'ward the rocky base the warrior sped

Aside he flung the gliding door,

Stepped lightly o'er the moss-grown floor,

Trod lightly on 'neath the crystal walls,

Far down the winding, echoing halls,
Past sparkling founts whose endless flow,
Fell 'neath the light of a mystic glow;
Stept lightly on through high arched walls,
Through white and shining marble halls;
Stept lightly down 'neath the castle dome,
Through the deep rotunda the sunlight shone
O'er glittering walls, where stalactites hung
Like gleaming jewels in the golden sun;
And the flowing founts, with splashing sound,
Filled the great depths of the cavern 'round.
Swift o'er the floor with noiseless sound,
The warrior leaped with hurried bound,
Spread with a light and gentle hand,
A fleecy couch on the shining sand;
Placed the sleeping form of the maiden fair,
'Mid the clinging folds of the ermine rare;
Where soft lights fell from the castle dome,
She lay like a queen on a royal throne.
Long he gazed on the sleeper fair,
On the waving flow of her trailing hair
On the pale young form as in a dream,
O'er the maiden's form the warrior leaned.

THE GREAT COHOES FALLS, MOHAWK RIVER, NEW YORK.

Far up the valley, the Mohawk vale,
The maid he bore through a sunny dale.

Then murmured in accents soft and low,

Like the sounding waters' rippling flow,

And his far off tones like sweet music fell,

O'er the sleeper's soul like a magic spell.

Beauteous maid! from thy magical scenes,

Float back thy bark from the distant streams.

From thy wild-wood haunts and thy forest home,

From thy leafy vales I bid thee come.

Long and steadily, with eyes intent,

O'er the sleeper's form the warrior bent,

With swaying arm and clap of hand,

He waved o'er her form his magic wand;

Then spoke, and his voice gave a thrilling sound

As it echoed long through the cavern 'round.

By all the powers of Unk-te-hee the great,

By all the powers opposed to fate,

Beauteous maid, from thy death-like sleep,

I bid thee wake, arise and speak!

Child of the midnight's stormy skies,

I bid thee speak, awake, arise!

Slowly and softly the maiden breathed.

A cloud of mist o'er the sleeper wreathed,

A sudden cry, a low, wild shriek,

And the maid half rose to her trembling feet.

With quivering sob and shuddering moan,

She reeled from her couch like a bird in storm;

With trembling hands and eyes upraised,

At the warrior chief the maiden gazed.

Then spoke, and the warrior's heart rejoiced,

At the dulcet tones the maiden voiced;

With far off look, as in a dream,

Her words fell soft as a murmuring stream.

Oh, Gitchee-man-ito! of earth and air,

Where am I, oh, Ogema, where am I, where?

Art spirit or mortal? do I behold

Man of my race, a warrior bold?

Or is it a fancy, a fleeting dream,

That thou art a friend? not a foe doth seem;

Thy face, like a god's, from a regal height,

Seems to wake my soul from the depth of night,

Wohon-o-win! wohon-o-win! woe is me, woe!

Speak, oh, Ogema, art thou friend or foe?

And the warrior smiled his kind intent,

As o'er her form he lowly bent;

Then murmured in tones like the sounding wave,

Like the singing wind through the winding cave:

Fear not, fair maid, from thy fevered dream
Awake, to the flow of the silvery stream,
To the birds' soft notes and the tinkling play
Of the rippling founts 'neath the misty spray;
Awake to the soundings of earth and air,
To the world's sweet music and sunshine fair.
And his words fell soft as the whispering breeze
That sighed aloft through the clinging leaves.
With quivering shudder and forward bound,
The maiden leaped o'er the shining ground,
Gazed far up through the castle dome,
Where the golden rays of the sunlight shone;
Then cried aloud in wondering awe,
As she reeled, half dazed, o'er the cavern floor—
Oh, the sun shines bright, the sky's serene,
My soul, were it all a strange, wild dream?
'Mid a fierce, dark cloud and the thunder's roar,
I dreamed I was borne from my native shore;
From the flowing streams by my wild-wood tent,
O'er fields and forests my course was bent,
On fierce, dark wings like a bird in flight,
I dreamed I was borne through the storms of
    night;

The wild winds roared, the lightnings played,
I dreamed, oh, Enah! I was afraid.
Yet still—be still, my trembling heart—
The paling shadows seemed to part,
And gleaming through the mist of night,
I dreamed I saw a strange, pale light;
Like a beacon star through the storm and gloom,
It shone through the depths of a vale called doom.
And a form—oh, a form of noble height—
Leaned o'er my couch in the hush of night
And whispered words my soul could hear,
Till my throbbing heart had ceased to fear.
A form, a form, oh, a form like thine,
Like an angel's soul it seemed to shine;
My heart was thrilled with the touch he gave,
Like a warrior chief he was bold and brave,
And his voice, like the sound of a music strain,
Sang to my soul a sweet refrain.
His voice, his voice, On-away, my heart!
And the maiden sprang with a sudden start,
Gazed at the warrior with bated breath,
As her face grew white as the face of death;
Her faltering lips breathed forth a sigh

The warrior heard, as it fluttered nigh.

His voice, his voice, oh, his voice seemed thine,

Yes thine, she murmured, the voice was thine;

And the crimson sprang to her ashy cheek,

As the fair young maid essayed to speak.

Long the warrior gazed at the maiden fair,

At her drooping eyes and trailing hair,

Then strode a space with measured tread,

In murmuring voice he softly said:

Thou art fair as a lily, fair as a dream,

Like the stars in their beauty thy bright eyes
  seem,

Thy innermost soul, like a jewel rare,

Shines through the casket pure and fair.

Beauteous maid, fair goddess, fair queen,

'Twas a vision thou saw, think not 'twas a dream

From which thou doth wake like a bird in the
  morn,

Like a fluttering bird from the wind and the
  storm.

Thou wert borne from thy home at midnight's
  lone hour,

When a dark evil demon held thee in his power;

Great Wakin-yan-tanka bore thee in the night,
On his great evil wings, at a far distant height;
Bore thee, fair maid, from thy loved mother's
    sight,
Bore thee to his vale, to the valley of gloom,
To the valley of evil, the valley of doom.
In the dark of the night when evil reigned round
    thee,
'Twas there in the gloom, in the shadows, I found
    thee.
A fair, sacred spirit, a daughter of night,
Led my wandering steps by a strange beacon
    light,
Deep in the vale 'neath spells that had bound
    thee,
Fair maid in thy beauty, enah, there I found
    thee,
Like a lily asleep, with the dew on its breast,
Like a fair drooping lily I found thee at rest.
Long in great wonder I gazed at thy form.
And asked of my soul from whence wert thou
    borne?
Till the fair sacred spirit of knowledge and light,

Answered my soul through the depths of the night;
Answered my soul like the singing of water,
Thou wert Wakin-wo-halpa, a sacred gift daugh-
ter.
Borne through the rays of a swift meteor light,
'Mid the swift Wakan-denda from far distant
height;
Thou wert born a fair goddess, a sacred gift star,
A sacred born daughter to Minne-ha-ha:
Named by the spirits Bright Minnewaska,
To the fair Queen of Beauty thou wert born her
fair daughter.
Like soundings of music the spirit voice fled,
And my soul in strange vision saw thee instead;
Saw thy fair form 'mid the storm of the night,
Borne from thy home in swift hurried flight;
'Mid Wakin-yan-tanka's dark wings outspread,
With thee, 'mid the darkness he floated o'er head.
Floated with thee to the deep depths of doom,
Down to the depths of the valley of gloom;
Long in the silence and hush of the night,
I gazed on thy form 'neath a strange mystic light;
At thy form as it lay 'neath the glimmer and shine,

I vowed I would woo thee, would wed thee as
mine;
And uttered fond words thy deep soul could hear,
Till thy answering heart had ceased from thy
fear;
Till thou yearned for the love my fond heart could
give,
And I knew by thy smile my own soul could live.
Scarce had I uttered this vow to my heart
When a loud, mocking laugh arose through the
dark,
And Wakin-yan-tanka, with great wings out-
spread,
Leaned o'er thy form with his dark looks of dread;
Breathed o'er thee his fierce blasting breath,
And vowed he would wed thee in life and in
death.
Ho! like a panther enraged to the fight,
I fought with my foe through the depth of the
night;
Fought for thee! for thee! Ne-ne-moo-sha my love,
Fought with the strength of the spirits above;
Fought with the foe the great god of thunder,

Fought with the strength, with the magic of
  wonder;
The great chieftain Mohonk, the son of my father
Fought with the strength of the great God of
  Water;
Fought till great Unk-te-hee leaned through the
  night,
Guided my aim, gave aid to the fight;
Gave magical aim till my arrow went speeding,
Till prone on the ground Wakin-yan-tanka lay
  bleeding;
Till pierced by my arrows the great God of
  Thunder
Lay stunned like the dead by the magic of wonder;
Till swift through the night with thee I went
  fleeing,
The great God of Thunder recovering, pursuing;
Till great An-pe-tu-wee the sun god, of yon height,
Pierced through his wings, his great wings of
  night;
Till reeling and rumbling like the mist of the morn
He vanished from sight through the shadows of
  dawn;

Till far up the Shawangunk my footsteps went
    leaping,
Till here 'neath my castle walls peacefully sleep-
    ing;
I woke thee, my love, Ne-ne-moo-sha, my queen,
I awoke thee! awoke thee! yet not from a dream;
I awoke thee, fair love, from enchantment's dread
    power,
From evil that bound thee, at midnight's lone
    hour;
From evil enchantment 'neath which thou wert
    bound,
I awoke thy calmed soul to the musical sound;
To the music of song-birds, the sweet sounds of
    the air,
To the world in its beauty and all that is fair.
I bid thy soul listen, hark! 'tis not a dream,
The melodious flow of the murmuring stream,
The brooklet's low murmur, the song birds in tune,
And the sound of the singing winds fanning the
    bloom.
Fair maid, lift thine eyes, 'neath the clap of my
    hand,

Let all sorrows disperse, 'neath the spell of my
    wand,

Let thy musical laughter resound in its mirth,

Let us roam far together, thou fairest of earth.

Fear not, oh, Me-tah-win, with magic of wonder,

I vanquished thy foe, the great god of thunder;

Unk-te-hee, the warrior, chief Mohonk, of the
    vale,

Bids thee follow him far, o'er his high mountain
    trail;

Fair maid, quick, thy hand, thou shalt roam like
    the wind,

Thou shalt dance through the forest, leap like a
    hind;

Quick from my castle walls see we are gliding,

Far up the mountain steep see we are striding,

Swift like the great eaglet soaring in flight,

We've reached the point of the steep mountain
    height;

Here 'neath the shade of the o'er-hanging trees,

We'll rest 'neath the cool of the soft summer
    breeze;

Rest from the dark, from the storms of the night,

'Neath great An-pe-tu-wee's fair, beauteous light.
See in the distance his golden rays gleam,
O'er deep running waters, o'er bright running
    stream,
O'er high hills and valleys, o'er forest and dale,
His great lights and shadows sweep over the vale,
Sweep over the forest tops, light winds are
    blowing,
Sweep o'er the forest tops far 'neath us flowing,
Deep in the shadows there leaps the young roe,
The ta-hinca-ska, the mountain deer, the fawn,
    and the doe,
The ta-hin-ca, the ta-to-ka, the tam-do-ka, the roe,
Swift as the shadows glide onward they go.
Lo, in the meadows there, 'neath the sun's gleam,
Flit the gay song-birds, 'neath the bright sheen,
The ape-chee, the so-so-kah, the chit-o-walk on
    the wing,
The owais-sa, the blue-birds, like jeebis they sing.
Fair maid, lift thine eyes, let their bright beauty
    gleam,
O'er the hills, the valleys, the swift running
    stream.

Far to the four winds, o'er the far-reaching plain,
The great chieftain Mohonk, holds magical reign.
The son of great Unk-te-hee holds at command
The rocks and the rivers, holds sway o'er the land,
Reigns the great chieftain, great Mohonk of the
    vale,
Leads his bold warriors, the Mohawks, on the
    trail;
Chief of the battle he leads to the fight,
Till all his great foemen fall neath his might.
Far as thine eyes can reach, far o'er the plains,
O'er the tribes of the Mohawk the great chieftain
    reigns.
Ho, the great Mohonk, with clap of the hand,
Will summon in strength all his brave warrior
    band;
I will send forth my signals till the echoes resound,
Till my warriors and allies rush forth to the sound.
See, in the distance like shadows they come,
List the faint sounds, 'tis the beat of the drum,
The beat of the tomtom, as swift from the dance,
They bring forth the quiver, the spear and the
    lance;

And the shouts of my warriors sound from the
    tepee,

As swift to my call they haste from the tee.

See, in the distance, my brave bands are trooping,

List their glad cries, their loud shouts, and their
    whooping.

Fair ma'd, ere my warriors and troops here
    assemble—

Withdraw not thy hand, why doth thou so trem-
    ble?

Ere my warriors have gazed on thy beauty so fair,

Let me twine this wreath in the shine of thy hair,

The drooping white lilies I plucked from the
    stream,

And crown thee, Me-tah-win, my bride and my
    queen.

Ne-ne-moo-sha, fair love, like the stars of the
    night,

Thou hast shed o'er my soul a sweet, witching
    light;

Like the stars in their beauty, oh, my love, oh,
    my queen,

Doth thine eyes in their beauty sparkle and gleam;

Let me sing at thy feet, oh, Mee-tah-win, my
  queen,
Let our hearts be united, like the swift running
  stream;
Let us roam hand in hand, like the flow of the
  river,
Let us join heart to heart forever and ever.

Long the warrior gazed with eyes intent,
O'er the maiden's form the warrior bent,
Then murmured in accents low and sweet,
Fair love, let thy soul to mine own soul speak.
Slowly and steadily, with eyes upraised,
At the warrior chief the maiden gazed,
Then spoke, and her voice like sweet music fell,
On the warrior's soul like a magic spell.
Oh, Ogema, oh, chieftain, of wonder and might,
To thee was I borne through the depth of the
  night;
Oh, Ogema, Ogema, of wonder and power,
To thee was I borne at midnight's lone hour.
To thee was I borne through the storms of the
  night,

By the great Gitchee-man-ito, the great spirit of
    light;
To thee, oh, mee-heen-yah, to thee was I borne,
Through deep depths of evil, through darkness
    and storm;
The great Gitchee-man-ito, the great giver of life,
Led me, oh, enah, through deep depths of strife.
Oh, Ogema, oh, Ogema, of wonder and might,
Thou'st sang to my soul like a spirit of light;
Thou'st sang to my soul till my heart in its singing,
Sounds to thine own in its musical ringing,
Till it leaps like a fountain, sings like a bird,
Echoes the music the breezes have stirred;
Echoes the love thy spirit hath brought me,
Echoes the love thy spirit hath taught me;
Soul of my soul, like the weak clinging vine,
My heart must ever around the entwine:
Soul of my soul, though the wild winds blow ever,
I am thine, oh, Ogema, oh, Mee-heen-yah, forever

     *   * *   *   *   *

Long the warrior gazed at the maiden fair,
At her shining eyes and streaming hair,
At her royal robes, that shone like dew,

Where the gleaming rays of the light shone
  through,
At a fair young form, lithe as a fawn,
At a face that shone like the light of dawn;
Long and silent, with look intent,
O'er the maiden's form the warrior bent,
Then raised her hand with a gentle grasp,
To his heart the willing maid he clasped.
Long and silent, as in a dream,
They stood like statues, like king and queen,
Like god and goddess, by magic bound,
'Neath the spell of love that reigned around.
Fast bound 'neath the spell of magical dreams,
They heeded naught of the fierce, wild scenes,
The sinking rays of the setting sun,
Or the gathering clouds that o'er them hung,
Fierce and wild through the fading light,
As they gathered force with the coming night.
Wrapped in the silence of deep love profound,
They heeded naught of the muttering sound—
A fierce, low rumble, of wings outspread,
As Wakin-yan-tanka wheeled high o'er head:
Whirled and circled, his huge form borne

High 'mid the winds of the on-rushing storm.
Whirling and circling, with great wings spread,
He leaned through the night with dark looks of
    dread—
Leaned o'er the lovers with fierce looks of ire,
As downward he aimed his swift darts of fire.
Swift from his talons, o'er his dark wings and
    under,
Swept the bright darts of the great God of
    Thunder,
Swept the red Wakindee, till great tongues of
    flame
Leaped through the forest, o'er valley and plain,
Sped the swift lightning, the great Wakindee
    light,
Till the dense forest blaze gleamed through the
    night;
Swift the red fire-light leaped from the ground,
Far up the mountain steep, circling them 'round,
Glowed the red forest flames round them and
    over,
O'er the fair, dreaming maid, o'er her fond lover,
As silent and motionless, not heeding a sound,

Silent and still, like statues of stone,
Stood the warrior and maiden, silent and lone,
Hand clasped in hand, heads bowed as if doomed
To the on-rushing flames that over them loomed.

They bowed to the spell 'neath which they were
    bound;

Lost to the night and the great danger 'round
    them,

Lost 'neath enchantment, 'neath the deep spell
    that bound them,

They heeded naught of the loud, mocking laugh-
    ter,

The loud mocking sounds that echoed long after,

As Wakin-yan-tanka, with flashings of light,

Flapped his huge wings and fled through the
    night;

Flapped his huge wings as he circled around,

And fled through the night with a rumbling sound.

Silent and still, like statues of stone,

Stood the warrior and maiden, silent and lone,

Hand clasped in hand, heads bowed as if doomed

To the on rushing flames that over them loomed.

Ho, like the Wakindee's swift flashing light,

The great God, Unk-tee-hee, leaned through the
    night,

Leaned through the misty clouds over him sway-
    ing,

Leaned thro' the dewy shrouds mistily straying,
Leaned o'er the glowing flames swiftly blowing,
Breathed forth the vapory clouds under him
    flowing;
Lo, to his breathing, his swift, mighty breathing,
Flowed forth the vapory clouds, whirling and
    wreathing.
Swift as the eaglet soaring homeward in flight,
The great God of Waters swept down through
    the night,
Swept o'er the mountain top, drifting thro' mist;
Swift the great Unk-te-hee leaned o'er the crest,
Leaned o'er the lovers, his great pinions of light
Enwrapped them like shields from the flames of
    the night.
Downward he leaned, then spoke soft and low,
Like the murmuring waves in their rippling flow,
Spoke to their souls, to the spirit that bound them,
As he spread his great mantle of magic around
    them.
Hark to my voice, oh, my son, oh, my daughter,
To the voice of great Unk-te-hee, God of earth
    and of water,

Afar from Ka-tha-ga, from my lodge in the west,
Afar o'er the pathway of ether and mist,
Afar o'er the pathway of the spirits of light,
Have I sought thee, my own, through the shades
    of the night.
Lo, in my soul have I heard thy sweet singing,
Thy voices' low chant, a rhythmical ringing,
As sounds forth the lute, as vibrates the harp,
So the spirit of love sings forth in thy heart:
Sings in thy heart, lo! thy two souls are plighted,
Lo! my children as one in love are united.
Fierce were the fates and evils that bound thee,
Long reigned the spirits of darkness around thee,
Brave is my warrior, who with magic of wonder,
Fought with my foe, the great God of Thunder.
Lo, from the raging flames surging around thee,
From the evils of fate, the evils that bound thee,
Lo, from fierce battle, from woe and from strife,
I will free thee forever, will give thee new life;
Will change thy two forms, thou shalt flow like
    a river,
Thou shalt be like the water, united forever;
Lo, thou art mine, my son and my daughter,

Thou shalt flow like the stream, like deep running water.

Deep as thy love will I delve thro' the mountain,

With my magical wand will I delve a deep fountain;

Down through the deep depths of unfathomable
space;

Thou shalt glide like a river, thou son of my race;

Thou son of great Unk-te-hee, thou son and thou
daughter,

Hand in hand thou shalt glide, like a river of water;

Thou shalt flow like a river, spring forth like a
fount,

As one thou shalt leap the steep sides of the
mount;

On neath thy shining robes downward shall glide,

The great chieftain Mohonk, Minnewaska his
bride—

As a musical fount, as a bright shining river,

United as one, thou shalt flow on forever

Swift as the Wah-kahn-dee's flashings of light,

Great Unk-te-hee leaned through the mist of the
night,

Reached forth his shining wand, glittering and
  gleaming,
Reached forth his magic hand, silently leaning;
High through the mountain top delved a deep
  fountain,
Reached forth his magic hand, delved through
  the mountain;
Deep through the mountain, through fathomless
  space,
A deep rocky cavern formed down thro' the base;
Reached forth his shining wand, leaning far over,
Touched with his magic hand the maid and her
  lover.
Lo, with a sounding shout, music and laughter,
The maid and her lover's form, changed into
  Vapor,
Changed to a shining cloud, mistily gleaming,
Swayed o'er the deep abyss, whirling and wreath-
  ing.
Swift the great Unk-te-hee breathed through the
  night,
And their cloud forms were changed to a river
  of light;

Sparkling and pure from the far distant height,

Flowed the bright emerald stream down through
 the night;

Down through the deep abyss, down through
 the mountain,

Leaped through the winding ways, sprang like a
 fountain,

Up o'er the mountain top, laughing with mirth,

Leaped o'er the rocky steep, downward to earth.

With music and laughter, o'er the steep mountain
 side,

Downward their spirit forms swayingly glide;

Dance through the misty foam, swaying in mirth,

They glide with a silvery stream far o'er the earth;

Far through the woodland, through forest and
 dale,

Like spirits of mist they glide through the vale;

Far o'er the valley, the river and tide,

O'er the great sea of water their spirit forms glide;

To and fro with gay laughter, with music and
 mirth,

They roam through the misty waves, gods of the
 earth:

MINNEWASKA FALLS, NEW YORK.

Fair 'neath the shining robes, flow like a fountain,
To and fro o'er the rocky side, down the steep mountain.

Fair 'neath their shining robes, flow like a foun-
tain,
To and fro o'er the rocky side, down the steep
mountain,
Leaping, dancing, laughing in mirth,
They glide with a silvery stream far o'er the earth.

* * * * * * * *

Afar to the eastward, o'er the hill and the vale,
Hath the spirit U-a-no-ma roamed far o'er the
trail,
Till here in thy valley, at thy feet, Minne-ha-ha,
These tidings I bring of thy fair Minnewaska.
Then sing, oh, sing! Oh, glad Minne-ha-ha!
Thou queen in thy beauty, oh, fair laughing
water;
Sing, oh, sing, till thy music and laughter
Go sounding through space and echoes long
after.
Sing when the night winds over thee sigh,
Sing when the storm clouds rages on high,
Sing when the night clouds over thee loom,
Then let thy pining heart cease from its gloom,
For lo, thy fair daughter, thy fair Minnewaska,

6 Minnewaska

Leaps to the sounds of the fair Laughing Water;
Leaps to the sounds of thy musical singing,
Leaps to thy echoes, to thy laughter and ringing,
Voicing thy laughter, thy music and mirth,
As she roams in her spirit form far o'er the earth.
Sing, oh, sing! oh, fair Minne-ha-ha!
Echo thy spirit voice far o'er the water,
Till with the sounding waves rhythmically ringing,
Minnewaska unites with thee, in her singing;
Leaping like thee, where the sunbeams stray,
Dancing in mirth neath the moonbeam's ray;
Flowing, swaying, plunging far downward,
Leaping, dancing, gliding far onward,
Till her sweet sounding voice, echoes to thee,
Afar o'er the winding ways, o'er earth and sea.
Lo, in the distance the night Sun of Light,
Han-ye-tu-wee, the waning moon, floats through
    the night,
Shrouding thy misty form, enwrapping thee
    'round;
'Mid deep shades and shadows, of mystery pro-
    found,
Far through the silent space, far thro' the night,

The moon's shade and shadows gleam far from
   yon height,
Afar through the silent space, leaning far o'er,
Her pale rays are beckoning me upward to soar;
Afar through the shadows the pale moon of night,
Beckons U-a-no-ma, her lone Daughter of Light;
Up through Wangee-ta-chan-ku, the spirit's path-
   way,
Will I glide through the misty path ere dawns
   the day,
Farewell, Minne-ha-ha, the moon's pinions of
   light,
Will bear me away through the shades of the
   night,
Bear me away to her bright realms afar,
Farewell Queen of Beauty, farewell Minne-ha-ha.

MISCELLANEOUS POEMS.

SCENES REMEMBERED.

Remembrance, sweet remembrance,
  Of life, when young and fair,
When my heart was ever singing,
  And my soul was free from care.
I remember a bright childhood,
  And a mother's sweet caress,
And a kind and loving father,
  Now numbered with the blest.

And, ah, yes, I remember
  A home down by the sea,
Where the waves were ever whispering
  Strange secrets to me,
As I listened to the dashing,
  And to the thund'rous roar,
And the washing and the rippling
  Of the waves along the shore.

I remember, I remember,
   When youth's glad hours had come,
How I roamed among the mountains
   Of a far and distant home,
Climbing with song and laughter,
   Up the rugged heights and steeps,
Trying the while with might and main
   For Shawangunk's topmost peaks.

There upon their lofty summits,
   To watch the waters flow
Through the lovely Wallkill valley,
   In the distance far below,
And view the misty storm clouds,
   As they gathered 'neath our feet,
And to see the rain drops falling
   To the valley far beneath.

There to watch the placid streamlet,
   Just before its mighty leap
Down the steep sides of the mountains,
   In one long and shining sheet,
To the valley in the distance,
   Through the valley far below—

There onward, calmly onward,
  Doth the Minnewaska flow.

And we pause quite oft to listen
  To the beating of the oar,
As it echoes and re-echoes
  Around Lake Mohonk's shore.
We reach to gather lichens,
  Along the rocky base
Of the steep, high walls that shut us in
  This strange, mysterious place.

Where the deep, dark waters sinking
  To a fathomless depth below,
Through the deep depths of the mountain,
  Do the hidden waters flow.
We could hear the dripping, dripping,
  And the plashing of the oar,
As it echoed and re-echoed,
  Around Lake Mohonk's shore.

I remember, I remember,
  Bold Hudson's lofty heights,
As we glided 'long the river,

Full many a starry night;
  Whilst the moon shone bright above us,
    And gleamed o'er the waves below,
  We watched the mystic shadows
    O'er the woodlands come and go.

Gliding, gliding onward,
  Far up the noble stream,
Where many bright and sparkling lights
  Along the shores gleam;
And the Highlands in their beauty,
  Deep, darksome shadows throw,
Of their great and massive grandeur,
  'Neath the waters far below.

I remember how we clambered,
  Ere the early dawn of light,
To view the glorious sunrise
  On Catskill's mountain height;
How in awe we stood there gazing
  On God's wondrous works divine,
And our hearts went out in praises,
  For nature's gifts sublime.

Lake Calhoun.

Beauteous lake! how merrily do thy waters dance
Along the glistening surface of thy wide expanse,
As though in rocking motions, rhythmic play,
Thou'd join the happy throngs that round thee stray,
As from dawn to dark along thy shores doth clatter,
The fleeting hoof, and merry children's patter.

CHARMING CALHOUN.

Beauteous lake! how merrily do thy waters dance
Along the glistening surface of thy wide expanse,
As though in rocking motions, rhythmic play,
Thou'd join the happy throngs that round thee
    stray,
As from dawn to dark along thy shores doth
    clatter,
The fleeting hoof, and merry children's patter.
Beauteous lake! how gaily doth thou thus em-
    brace,
The ever onward motion of the civilizing race,
And join in action, with joyous leap and bound,
The busy world that hails thy magic sound.

Doth wave kind welcome to the throngs that
    come and go,
As the winds are gently tossing thy waters to
    and fro,
Or do we in thy calmer motions trace
Thy non-forgetfulness of a long departed race?
Doth hear among the boughs that o'er thee sigh,
The whispered words and sounds of days gone by,

When by thy shores the red man made his dwell-
    ing place,
And grandly reigned a wild, romantic race?

There steals a quiet hush o'er the landscape round;
There's scarce a murmuring voice or disturbing
    sound,
To mar the peaceful beauty of the declining day,
As the soft zephyrs and sunbeams o'er thee stray.
And thy languid waves doth sink to rest,
'Neath the fierce heat of the sun's caress;
Calmly, serenely doth thy placid waters lay
'Neath the gleaming rays of the summer day.
The gay birds pipe their sweet, wild notes,
As o'er thy surface they skim and float,
Their light wings glance to the woods away,
To thy shores, bright Calhoun, where thy waters
    play.

Slowly, slowly the sun doth o'er thee glide,
Sinking in dazzling beauty beyond thy green hill-
    side,
Beyond thy western banks where still the tall
    trees grow,

Where time hath not yet laid their grandeur low;
Where still the woodbine's massive foliage
clings,
And the gay plumed bird, 'mid shadows, sits and
sings.
The sun hath set, how calmly doth thy placid
waters lay,
As though the gentle breeze had won thee from
thy play,
And had lulled thee to sweet repose and happy
dreams
Of other days and well remembered scenes;
And thou mayest now behold, as evening's dusk
descends,
The shades of countless forms that with the
shadows blend.

They come in their grandeur, tall and strong,
There are warriors bold and brave,
They pass thy woodland shores around,
In their warrior costumes 'rayed,
They march with slow, majestic steps along,
And vanish in the evening's mystic shade.

There are snow-white tents by thy wooded shores,
'Neath the verdant trees and bowers,
The curling smoke from their peak ascends,
Far up where the storm cloud lowers,
And round their birch bark tent there grows
Sweet scented buds and flowers.

There are dark eyed maids with loose bound hair,
And braves with their bow and spear,
They gallop away, o'er the hill tops far,
In chase of the fleeting deer,
And the maidens laugh, and wave and shout,
As their dark forms disappear.

There are mirthful sounds on the stilly air,
When in broidered mantles 'rayed,
The dusky maids come tripping down,
For a plunge 'neath thy cool blue wave,
And deck their hair by thy mirrored light,
For the dance with their warriors brave.

When at night they hear the tomtom's beat,
By the camp-fire's ruddy blaze,
And the deep red glow of the gleaming light,

Reflects o'er the silvery waves,

There the maids and warriors gather round,

And dance 'neath the moonbeams rays.

They trip with light, fantastic grace,

With shouts and laughter gay,

And step to wild and weird sounds,

Whilst the tomtoms beat and play,

Till the moon shines high in the star lit sky,

And fond lovers steal away.

They glide o'er the calm, still waters,

Whilst the moon goes floating by,

The lover wooes the dark-eyed maid,

'Neath the shine of the starry sky,

And leans upon his glistening oar,

As he bends for her low reply.

They are gliding, gliding onward,

Like birds they seem to soar,

And thy bosom beats to the measured stroke,

To the dip of the silvery oar,

As slowly, slowly, they float and fade,

Mid the shades of the distant shore.

The moon shines high in the starry sky,
And gleams o'er thy waters deep,
There's not a wave or ripple stirs
Thy bosom's restful sleep;
Dream on, dream on, whilst yet thou may,
Whilst silence reigns complete.

List, the whispering winds have changed
To a dull and sullen roar;
The whirling leaves are flying fast,
On the sands along the shore,
And mid the heavens, high o'erhead.
The storm clouds gather o'er.

The wind comes whistling, shrieking on,
The tall trees rock and sway,
The thunder's deafening crash is heard,
Where the lightnings flash and play.
Still on, and on, the storm hath burst,
Where thy placid waters lay.

And thy calm bosom heaves, rolls and wakes,
Dashing in surging waves and foaming flakes

Against thy storm-tossed shores, doth heave and
    moan,
The tear sprays dashing 'mid the misty foam;
Thy happy visions fade of the departed past,
Sighing wakes, e'en thy dreams, too beautiful to
    last.

There are mutterings in the distance, where the
    storm hath past,
There are rays of light ascending o'er the heavens
    vast,
And many sounds are heralding the near ap-
    proach of day,
As the darkness o'er the hill-tops slowly fades
    away,
The light advances onward and o'er thy waters
    glide,
Whilst anon thy heavings, in restfulness, subside.

The sun rides up in glory and o'er thee sheds his
    beams,
His warmth and radiance o'er thy glistening sur-
    face streams,

All thy moist and misty tear-sprays are being
  kissed away,
As the great and mighty monarch rings up the
  coming day,
And gazing on his glory thou'st quite forgot thy
  dream,
Of thy old, departed grandeur, where nature
  reigned supreme.

The day rolls on in beauty, soft zephyrs round
  thee stray,
The sun and winds hath won thee to mingle with
  their play,
And thou art gayly leaping and dancing on the
  shore,
As gleefully and merrily as in the days of yore,
Till the leafy boughs at evening wave o'er thee
  to and fro,
And thy rippling waters, with their shadows,
  come and go,

Till the sun rolls down, and o'er thee, in bough,
  and bush, and tree,
The birds are sweetly singing their vesper songs
  to thee,

Till the evening zephyrs murmur, till the evening
   breezes blow,
Rocking, gently rocking, thy waters to and fro.
Beauteous lake, how calmly doth thou sink to
   rest,
With the splendors of the setting sun reflecting
   o'er thy breast.

TO THE HUDSON.

Flow on noble Hudson, flow on in thy pride,
Matchless in beauty, flow on thou swift tide,
Flow on through thy valleys, thy uplands and
   heights,
Flow on whilst thy bosom reflects the bright lights
Of the gay, dancing sunbeams, as o'er thee they
   glide,
Flow on, noble river, flow on in thy pride.

Flow on, noble river, flow on in thy power,
Whilst thy great hills above thee in grandeur
   doth tower,
Like a great, mighty army, to shield all thy length,

They stand in their boldness, their beauty and
strength;
Flow on whilst o'er thee thy noble hills tower,
Flow on, noble river, flow on in thy power.

Flow on, noble Hudson, in thy splendor sublime,
Flow on forever, flow on for all time,
Whilst each and all nations unite in thy praise,
Exalting thy grandeur, thy beauty, thy waves;
Flow on, noble Hudson, in thy splendor sublime,
Flow on noble river, flow on for all time.

THE NAVESINK RIVER.

Down by the Navesink River,
Down by the silvery stream,
Was nestled our little cottage,
Mid banks of the rarest green.

Can I e'er forget my childhood,
And that dear old home of mine,
Where the flowers bloomed the rarest,
And the dear old ivy twined.

How oft I've sat on the hill-side,
And watched the waves at play,
As they chased and chased each other,
And floated far away.

Oft times at the close of evening,
I've wandered by the shore,
And I've heard the whip-poor-wills singing,
Far up in our old sycamore.

But now I know I've been dreaming
Of the home I'll ne'er see more,
Of the home I loved in my childhood,
Down on the Navesink shore.

TO THE WOODS AWAY.

Come, oh, come, to the woods away,
Come, oh, come, to the hills to-day,
Come, for my heart is light and free,
Come, for my heart is dreaming
Of the golden sunlight, streaming
    O'er hill and lea.

Come, in the spring's early dawn,
Come, ere the dew from the rose is gone,
And roam o'er the fields away;
Come, where the brooklet, murmuring flows,
Come, where the wild-wood violet blows,
    And sweet zephyrs play.

Come, list to the song-birds singing
Mid tall tree branches swaying
O'er some clear stream;
Come, for my heart is dreaming
Of the golden sunlight streaming
    O'er meadows green.

— —

WHIP-POOR-WILL.

As I wander afar through the evening shade,
Afar o'er the hilltops and down through the glade,
I hear from the hedge, with a strange, wild thrill,
The sad, plaintive call of the whip-poor-will.
    Whip-poor-will, whip-poor-will, whip-poor-will.

And my mind swiftly turns to a time long ago,
When in childhood I wandered at eve to and fro,

With a father's strong hand tightly grasping my
   own,
I hear his voice echo, in soft under-tone,
As I wander to-night in the shades here alone.
   Whip-poor-will, whip-poor-will, whip-poor-will.

And I think when I hear that low, plaintive sound,
My father, in spirit, is hovering around,
And I hear the low echo his mellow tones made,
As they sound o'er the hilltops and down through
   the glade.
   Whip-poor-will, whip-poor-will, whip-poor-will.

AUTUMN LEAVES.

Listen to the leaflets falling,
   Downward they are borne,
And the winds are softly sighing,
   Autumn days have come.
We shall miss them, miss them, miss them,
   And their verdure form,
When the naked boughs are bending
   'Neath the winter's storm.

They are murmuring, softly murmuring,
  In their downward flight,
As their tender leaves are falling,
  'Neath the sun's warm light.
Thus it is with youth and beauty,
  Born like the rose at dawn,
Ere the harsher winds have chilled them.
  Earthward they are borne.

Listen to their sighing, sighing,
  Rustling in their flight,
Withered leaves are falling, falling,
  Neath the frost and blight.
"Thus it is ere man hath distanced
  Half his span of life,
He sinks beneath life's care and burden,
  Downward in the strife."

But our hearts are list'ning, list'ning,
  To a happier tale,
Where the bright hued leaves are glist'ning
  In the sun-lit dale,
Where the leaves fall in their beauty,
  Youth and age alike,

Tinted with the wands of heaven,
    'Neath its mellow light.

Falling, falling, gently falling,
    Bright hued leaves aglow,
Downward in their flight of beauty,
    Murmur as they go,
"Death is but the earthly ending
    Of life's fleeting show,
Richer far are colors blending,
    In the afterglow."

THE DEATH OF SUMMER.

Fair summer lies in the valley,
    Lies peacefully asleep,
And song-birds sweetly warbling,
    Chant requiems at her feet.

All perished now and withered,
    Are the garlands that she strew,
All the lilies and the roses,
    The bright flowers wet with dew.

The rills and gliding rivulets,
Lie bound 'neath icy chains,
The dazzling King of Winter
O'er beauteous Summer reigns.

Placed are his robes around her,
White shrouds of fleecy snow;
O'er the form of gentle Summer,
The wild winds fiercely blow.

Beneath cold Winter's covering,
Fair Summer calmly dreams
Of opening flowers and blossoms,
And purling brooks and streams.

Of Spring's footsteps, softly gliding
O'er her frozen shrouds of snow,
And the spirit of fair Summer,
Wafts where soft breezes blow.

THE DESERTED HOME.

Yes, here is the home where in childhood we've
    played,
And here the green elms still throw their dense
    shade,
And here on these banks, where the moss grows
    so green,
I've played with my brothers beside this clear
    stream.

Yes, here we've wandered in childhood's bright
    hours,
And here we've gathered the sweetest of flowers,
No rose ever bloomed on its green, nodding
    stem,
That e'er could compare in fragrance to them.

No bird ever warbled a song or a trill,
That could cause our young hearts with such
    pleasure to thrill,
No vine ever twined up a rocky, steep face,
That could fall with more airy or negligent
    grace.

Where now are those brothers that roamed by
   my side,
Who in youth were our joy, our dear mother's
   pride?
One buried from home, afar out at sea,
And one lies with sweet mother, neath our green
   elm tree.

I'll never again hear their glad, ringing shout,
Never again hear their glad songs ring out,
Our home is deserted, our loved ones all fled,
E'en the green verdure lies withered and dead.

Oh, the sun does not shine o'er our home any more,
Shut is our gate, and locked is our door,
The tall trees are casting deep shades of gloom,
And all, all is shadowed with death and the tomb.

SLEEP.

Come, sweet Sleep, I love thee well,
Come, with thy strange and witching spell;
Come, with thy sweet and happy dreams,
And waft me by beautiful, silvery streams.

Come, sweet Sleep, I woo thee to-night,
Come with dreams of all things bright;
Come with music in cadence low,
Swelling and swelling as on we go.

Come, sweet Sleep, I woo thee now,
Come, chase care from my weary brow;
Come, waft me up in castles of air,
That I may forget all sorrows there.

Come, with thy beautiful dreams so rare,
Come, show me all things pure and fair;
Come, with visions of all things pure,
And tell me 'twill ever, forever endure.

RAIN.

Listen to the rain drops falling,
Dripping, dropping o'er the pane,
And the gushing, and the rushing,
And the rippling of the rain.

How it patters o'er the roof tops,
Tapping low a sweet refrain,
As we list to memory's echo,
Coming with the sounding rain.

Bringing back our childhood's pleasure,
Bringing back its joys again,
As our thoughts are backward turning,
Listening to the beating rain.

Bringing back our old time friendships,
Bringing thoughts of home again,
As we listen to the dripping
And the falling of the rain.

How it patters, patters, patters,
Down the hillside, through the lane;
Leaping, dancing, mid the pebbles,
Onward flows the joyous rain.

And the rustling of the leaflets,
Murmuring welcome as it came,
With the flowerets' bending petals,
Lifting, sips the pearly rain.

Foaming brooklets swell with laughter,
Rippling o'er with mirth again,
As o'er rocks, through defiles plunging
Downward with the rushing rain.

Sings aloud the vales and woodlands,
Sings aloud the verdant plain,
As the rills and rivulets dances
Downward, 'neath the falling rain.

SONGS OF MAY.

Oh, welcome, welcome, merry May,
With blossoms sweet and fair,
There's beauty in the valleys now,
And wild blooms scent the air.

There are song-birds in the forest,
Where rippling brooklets play,
And happy hearts are thrilled again,
With sounds of merry May.

Then welcome, welcome, merry May,
With footsteps light and free,
There's gladness in thy joyous reign,
All nature smiles for thee.

There are meadows strewn with violets,
Where romping children play,
And happy hearts attuned with song,
To welcome merry May.

Bring flowers, bright flowers,
Strew where thy footsteps roam.

BRING FLOWERS.

Bring flowers, fresh flowers,
Oh, glorious, beautiful Spring,
Let glorified angels imbue in our hearts,
The odors that round them cling.

Bring flowers, sweet flowers,
From purified bowers above,
That passionate hearts that o'er them bend,
May breathe sweet thoughts of love.

Bring flowers, pure flowers,
Thou gentle spirit of spring;
Bring palms, bring lilies, on Easter morn,
To crown our Lord and King.

Bring flowers, rare flowers,
Strew o'er Mount Calvary's cross,
For there hath our Savior in agony died,
For perishing souls that are lost.

Bring flowers, spring flowers,
Deck earth with brightest bloom,
Let all earth smile 'neath their fragrant bowers,
Rejoice 'neath their sweet perfume.

Bring flowers, bright flowers,
Strew where thy footsteps roam,
That beautiful emblems of peace and love,
May brighten each heart and home.

THE AFTERGLOW.

The sun hath set beyond
    the banks afar,
And where the golden orb hath shone there gleams
    a lonely star,
Glistening and scintilating like some
    rare gem
Set mid the golden lights of the world's
    bright diadem.

Crimson, purple and gold streak
    the night's horizon,
Till fold, on fold, the splendors of
    their mingled lights together roll,
The reflecting sheen nearing the goal
Of heaven's own beauty.

So the golden orb of day
    hath shed her crown,
To be renewed at morrow's dawn,
Like some blest soul who takes his
    heavenly flight
Through the dark corridors of
    shadowy night,
And gliding on o'er death's
    mysterious stream,
Doth leave to earth the afterglow
Of the soul—redeemed.

IN REALMS OF THOUGHT.

There's a beautiful realm that the soul can trace,
Like the light-winged birds through aerial space,
And tho' bound by chains the fates have forged,
With tightening bonds our lives to scourge,
We'll bid adieu to the tyrant race,
And out from the gloom of their biding place,
We'll flit away with our thoughts so free,
They fain would journey with us and see
The smiling meadows, the sunlit sea,
And the beautiful lands where thoughts are free

Oh, beautiful lands, where all joys are found,
With rapture we'll onward and onward bound,
To havens of sunlit isles of rest,
Where friends meet friends with love's caress.
The loved and parted here too are found
Journeying onward, homeward bound,
And we seem to see the gates ajar,
Where our loved and parted have crossed the bar;
Oh, sweet are these visions, with rapture fraught,
As we glide from the world in realms of thought.

Away, away, with all care and strife,
We've roamed to lands where joy is rife,
And charmful, magical sounds we hear
Of seraphic songs and gladsome cheer;
And the mellowing lights of eve are flung
O'er the choral bands where their harps are strung;
And we seem to hear in the distance far,
A welcoming voice like a guiding star,
Signaling us out from the spheres of night,
Out from the shades into seas of light.

In thoughts away to these lands we'll soar,
Sweet are the beauties we'll now explore,

To far off valleys our feet have strayed;
We lay our forms 'mid the cooling shade,
And list to the chorus the song-birds sing,
As adown the valleys their echoes ring;
And the sweet, loved voices of friends now gone,
Come floating like music the vales along,
Our souls are thrilled as our hands are clasped
By these white-robed figures as they pass.

Oh, spirits of Beauty, eternal, sublime,
Like stars set in spheres of endless time,
Would we could follow Thee out of our night,
Into Thy realms of endless light.
Guide our thoughts upward and onward we pray,
Past the rough shoals where our feet would stray,
Into Thy realms of unity;
Past the dark portals of life's troubled sea,
Into Thy glorious eternity.

THE INNER LIGHT.

There's a temple gray in the forest wilds,
And a bright light gleams through its vestal
    aisles,
Shedding its rays like a gleaming star
Through the deep night shades and gloom afar;
And a pilgrim, strayed from his path aright,
Turned his wandering steps t'ward the beacon
    light.

He seeks admittance from cold and storm,
Where the temple fires shine bright and warm,
And the inner lights through the temple stream
O'er the way-worn soul with a sacred gleam;
And bending low in a silent prayer,
The storm-tossed soul finds shelter there.

Still the beacon shines through the shadows dim,
As the bells peal forth the vesper hymn,
Chants the sweet welcome, soft and low,
Where the inner lights of the vestal glow;
And the soul's bathed pure 'neath a flood of light
That flows through the temple, soft and bright.

THE OLD CABIN HOME.

Turned him t'ward the old log cabin,
Where his children romp and roam.

Slowly wending through the pathway
Led him lowing oxen home.

THE OLD CABIN HOME.

Fair were the waving fields and forests,
  Sang the gay birds on the bough,
Cheerfully whistling in the meadows,
  Trod the farmer at his plow.
Like a shadow in the distance,
  Nestling mid the wood and vine,
Stood the farmer's old log cabin,
  Browned with age, defying time.

O'er the hill-tops to the westward,
  Slowly sank the setting sun,
And the farmer turned his plow-share,
  Glad his toilsome work was done;
Turned him t'ward the old log cabin,
  Where his children romp and roam,
Slowly wending through the pathway,
  Led his lowing oxen home.

Many were the sounds of greeting,
  As he passed the gateway through,
Loud and merry cries of children,
  And the cattle's welcome low.
Dusky seemed the old log cabin,

Standing mid the shadows round,
But within the fire-light gleaming,
 Showed where love and rest were found.

Gathered in the old log cabin,
 At the waning of the day,
Gleaming through the dusk of evening.
 Beamed the candle's fitful ray,
Bright and shining o'er the faces,
 Smiling out amid the gloom,
Father, mother, sons and daughters
 Happy in their humble home.

Lithe and blooming were the maidens,
 Treading o'er the puncheon floor,
And their bright and sturdy brothers,
 Gleefully wrestling at the door.
There were merry jests and laughter.
 Frolicsome little ones at play,
Dancing 'mid the song and music,
 As they whiled the hours away

Smiling and kind the mother,
 Seated at the frugal meal,

Beckoning all the group about her,
   Showing reverence they feel,
As with solemn voice the father
   Bends his head above the board,
Offering up his glad thanksgiving,
   For the bounty of the Lord.

Hard and rugged are the sinews
   Of the toiler's brawny arm,
Long and rough has been his labor,
   Pioneer of home and farm;
But his glance beams proud contentment,
   And his laugh resounds with mirth,
Though his home be e'er so humble,
   There is peace about the hearth.

From such homes have sprung our heroes,
   Cultivating soul and brain,
Round by round they struggled upward,
   To the pinnacles of fame.
Toiled and fought for home and country,
   Pressing forward in the fray,
Strong of heart they toiled and labored,
   For sweet home and liberty.

From such homes came martyred Lincoln,
  Emancipator, good and true,
And many of our noblest leaders,
  Who led our fearful battles through.
All honor to the old log cabin,
  And the honest laborer at his toil,
Faithful and true to home and country,
  Honest, faithful, true and loyal.

——— ————

SPRING.

Awake in the morn's early dawning,
And gaze from the lattice pane,
The roses and flowers are blooming,
Fresh after the early spring rain.

Awake to the birds' early tuning,
As they sing and sway on the bough;
Awake, dream not of dull sadness,
Chase care from thy wearisome brow.

Come join with the birds in their tuning,
As they merrily warble in glee,

The roses and flowers are blooming,
Fair nature smiles welcome for thee.

Awake in the morn's early dawning,
Let songs ring joyous and free,
There's a joy and balm in kind nature,
She waves her glad greetings to thee.

FAIR LAND OF DREAMS.

How oft in waking visions
In thy fair sweet land of dreams,
Have we wandered through thy flowery vales,
By thy gently winding streams.
Oh, regal are thy pillared halls,
And fair thy domes of light,
And shining are the steps that lead,
All gleaming marble white,
That lead our fancy up and on
To realms of pure delight.

Away with earthly care and pain,
Away with toil and strife,
We'll mount the ladder fair heights to gain,

We'll mount where pleasure holds high reign;
We'll stem the billows, ford the tide,
In Elysian's harbor safe we'll glide,
And view thy beauteous plane:
We'll rise o'er mounts that roll between,
And sweetly, idly, rest and dream.

What visions rise, what dreams replete,
What hopes, ambitions, joys complete,
What mighty works, and goals well won,
What noble deeds, and kind acts done,
What future efforts, and goals to win,
What fair, sweet hopes, come gliding in.

Ill fate is vanquished, we have no fears,
We're done with sorrows, done with tears,
Just drifting on, with kind fate to guide,
With faith and love close by our side.
Just drifting past the might have been,
Past old mistakes, folly and sin,
Past vanished hopes and dead days gone,
T'ward the roseate glow of a future dawn,
To the summer slopes, 'mid effulgent beams,
We'll find respite in the land of dreams.

DAWN.

A spirit came out of the misty dawn,
    Came up o'er the shadowy way,
And whispered the curtain would soon be drawn
    On the birth of another day.

Swiftly the mystic shades rolled on,
    Rolled on through realms of space,
And the king of morn was swiftly borne
    Up over the darkened waste.

Up, up, he rides, 'mid aerial heights
    He shines through realms of blue,
Shedding his glorious rays of light,
    His lances glancing through.

King of the morn, king of the noon,
    King of the brilliant day,
All earth is thrilled beneath thy touch,
    And hails thee on thy way.

The woodbird sitting 'neath the boughs,
    Unfolds its wings and sings;
The gladdening cry of nature lifts,
    And upward, upward rings.

King of the morn, king of the noon,
  King of the living day,
Slowly, slowly thou art gliding on,
  Till thy beams are merged with gray.

Gliding in royal splendor down,
  Down, down 'mid shades of night;
Again the banners o'er thee stream
  In gold and crimson light.

Thus sinks the king of morn and noon,
  Thus sinks the king of day,
The darkening shades of night are thrown
  Around him where he lay.

Glide on, glide on, thou monarch king,
  Glide on, glide on thy way,
Again at dawn shall thou be born,
  To chase the night away.

IN THE TWILIGHT.

In the twilight, evening twilight.

When the stars come gleaming through,

When the moon shines in her beauty,

'Tis then, my love, I dream of you.

In the twilight, evening twilight.

My heart forever sings of thee;

When the evening shadows linger,

I dream, fair love, I dream of thee,

I dream, fair love, I dream of thee.

When the evening shadows ling'ring,

Bathe the blooming flowers with dew,

And the bird songs, sweetly blending,

Speaks, fair love, fair love of you.

When the pure white lilies bending,

Floating on the silvery stream,

All their fairy fragrance lending,

'Tis then of thee, of thee I dream.

MOONLIGHT.

'Twas midnight's lone hour,
Dreaming there in my bower,
Alone in my bower elysian;
The moon, shining down,
Seemed to smile where she hung,
Seemed to smile at my strange, wild delusion.

At my fancy so fraught
With the spell of the night,
With the spell of her beauty ethereal;
I felt I could live 'neath the spell of her light,
Live for aye, 'neath a spell so aerial.

At midnight's lone hour,
Neath my vine-covered bower,
Like the fragrance of incense ascending,
Arose the perfume of the lily and rose,
'Mid the night air, so charmingly blending.

'Mid the night winds' low tone,
As I dreamed there alone,
Alone with the stars o'er me shining,
I thought I were blest,

Could I lie there and rest
For aye, 'neath my dream bower reclining.

But morn broke the spell,
And I heard the sad knell,
Knew my beautiful dream lights were fading,
Saw the moon's waning light
Fade away with the night,
Saw her smile a farewell at my waking.

DRIFTING.

My ships are drifting o'er the sea,
As the light of hope drifts far from me,
One by one they are sailing out
Into the shadows of mist and doubt.

The ships of childhood swift wave tossed
Amid the reefs of the past are lost;
Each white winged barque wrecked far at sea,
Will ne'er again return to me.

Youth's fair ship, with its precious store,
Drifts, drifts away from the sunlit shore,

Lightly they bound o'er the crested tide,
Those fleeting ships of our joy and pride.

Through the bright sea waves and raging storm,
In the distance far my ships are borne,
Past many a shoal each floating barque
Drifts, drifts away in the storm and dark.

Oh, the winds blow high, and the sea waves roar,
My drifting ships return no more;
'Mid the surging waves they're lost from view,
Farewell, my barque, adieu, adieu!

Mayhap they'll reach some far off clime,
As they drift adown the isles of time;
Far, far away o'er the sunlit sea,
Mayhap my barque may beckon me.

A WINTER NIGHT VISION.

I leaned at the pane one wintry night,
And watched the clouds as they sailed in sight,
My soul was filled with rapturous awe,
At the strange and wonderous sight I saw;
Out from the misty clouds of night,
Came throngs on throngs of angels bright.

It seemed like a vision of All-Saints' Day,
As they knelt at a great white throne to pray,
Then seemed to rise with majestic mien,
And string their harps to some hallowed strain,
Then onward took their heavenward flight,
Away, away, through the realms of night.

Like majestic spirits robed in white,
Slowly, slowly gliding from sight,
A beautiful, radiant, happy band,
Seeking a better, fairer land;
Like beautiful souls redeemed for aye,
Gladly, joyously they float away.

On, on they go, where, who can tell?
But list, I hear no parting knell,
Yet they seem to wave a last farewell

To the snow-bound earth, where they used to dwell,
And seem to shout, in glad delight,
We're done with earth, good night, good night.

Whilst 'neath them in the earth below,
Glistens and gleams the pure white snow,
The pure white snow, like a bridal veil,
Robing woodland, hill and dale,
Covering cottage, roof and peak,
Where the inmates lie, all wrapped in sleep.

Shrouding city, roof and dome,
Where lights and shadows go and come;
Where rifts on rifts of clouds sweep by,
All bathed in the light of the star-lit sky;
Still slowly, silently, they fade from sight,
Fade away in the shades of night.

But the beautiful clouds all melt away,
I wake from my dream, 'tis break of day,
And the beauteous forms of seraphs bright,
Have returned to mist, vanished from sight,
The moon shines on in the calm, blue sky,
She hath bidden her radiant guests good-bye.

BIRTHDAY GREETINGS.

Oh, our fond hearts doth greet thee,
  With wishes warm and true,
That each returning year may bring
  All happiness to you.

Oh, that the dove of peace may reign
  Within thy walls for aye,
And that the light of love may stream
  Forever o'er thy way.

And may thy cares like shadows fade,
  And vanish 'neath the tide,
And may kind fortune's laden barque
  Within safe harbor glide.

Oh, may return of many years,
  Bring rest from care and sorrow,
And may thy thankful heart give praise,
  For the coming of the morrow.

WHAT THE WINDS SAY.

Hark, hear the wild winds sweeping,
   Up through the murky sky,
And down through vales and lowlands,
   Hear them sweeping by.

Listen, hear the beating
   And plashing of the rain
Against the close shut casement,
   And o'er the dripping pane.

Hear the wild winds shrieking
   And sighing at the door,
It's some wild tale they're uttering,
   And whispering o'er and o'er.

What are the wild winds saying,
   As they sob and moan and sigh?
What are the wild winds saying?
   List to their plaintive cry.

A mighty power hath cast us out
   From a mysterious realm,
We have no will to guide our course,
   No anchor, rudder, helm.

138

Though winged through space we onward fly,
　Steered by an unseen hand,
We're sent to roam o'er many seas,
　And o'er the world's fair land.

We stir the deepest, darkest seas,
　With our awful might and power;
We toss the heaving billows up
　To where the storm-clouds lower.

The great waves rolling onward,
　Dash o'er the reef-bound shore,
We bear the sounds upon our wings
　Of the ocean's mighty roar.

Of the ocean's heaving, bounding,
　With sullen, roaring moan,
Of vessels leaping, tossing on,
　Amid the seething foam.

Of men's voices hoarsely calling,
　As in vain their helm they veer,
Help, help! we're drifting, drifting,
　And their cheeks grow pale with fear.

Drifting, drifting, drifting,
  On toward the rock-bound shore,
Their wildly ringing shouts for aid,
  Are resounding o'er and o'er.

The raging billows rolling up,
  From out the surging deep,
Plunge o'er the rocking vessels,
  With a mighty roar and leap.

A thousand voices rend us
  With piercing cries and shrieks,
As their struggling forms are swept away,
  Shrouded 'neath the deep.

And the tolling, tolling, tolling
  Of wild bells still you'll hear,
'Mid the soundings of our storm winds,
  As we are sweeping near.

We caught their echoing dirges,
  As they wafted to and fro,
Where the sinking vessels drifted
  With the water's ebb and flow.

We've swept o'er hills and mountains,
    And where the storm-clouds meet,
And o'er the lands of earth afar,
    And through the rolling deep.

And 'mid the lights and shadows,
    And 'mid the hill and vale,
And o'er the ocean's bounding tide,
    There comes a mighty wail

Of human souls bowed down in grief,
    With sorrows burdened o'er,
With soul's bowed 'neath oppression's yoke,
    To rise again no more.

We are bearing o'er sea and land,
    Their bitter, moaning cry,
And on our wings there lingers yet
    Sad nature's plaintive sigh.

Wild winds, wild winds, rush onward,
    Rush on with moaning cry,
The human heart grows faint with dread,
    As thou art passing by.

Oh, subtle are the ruling powers,
　That guide thy onward course,
That guide thee on and on through space,
　Long wandering, yet not lost.

Go then, whirling on thy way,
　Bearing weal and woe alike,
The powers that guide thy onward flight,
　Will lead thy course aright.

　　*　　*　　*　　*　　*　　*　　*

List, there comes a lulling pause,
　The sobbing winds have changed,
They whisper of their wanderings
　O'er sunny hills and plains.

Light winds are passing onward,
　Softly as whispering dreams,
They are murmuring of rippling brooks,
　Of smoothly gliding streams.

They are passing, passing onward,
　List what the light winds say,
List what the light winds whisper,
　As they gently round us play.

We've roamed o'er snow-capped mountains,
　Where gleams the northern star,
And where the palmy branches wave
　O'er eastern lands afar.

And through the woodland forests,
　And o'er the western plain,
We've bowed tall, waving grasses
　Before us as we came.

We've roamed o'er sunny southland,
　Where spicy blossoms blow,
Where the citron and the orange waft
　Their fragrance to and fro.

We've swept beneath the shadows
　Of the evening's drooping shade,
And dipped the rippling waters,
　As we lingering with them played.

Then on, and on, and onward,
　O'er hills and valleys through,
We've sprayed the blooming flowers
　With the ever cooling dew.

And on our wings there lingers yet
   The perfume of sweet flowers,
The warbling of the merry birds
   Amid their leafy bowers.

The murmuring of the gushing brook,
   The rustling of bush and tree,
As gently through the forest floats,
   Our light winds, gay and free.

    *   *   *   *   *   *   *   *

Light winds, light winds, thrice welcome,
   To thy cool breeze wafting by,
Thou'st fanned to rest the pulsing breast,
   That throbs 'neath the burning sky.

Oh, gentle winds thou'st whispered where
   Burdens of sorrow roll;
Thou'st borne the breath of hope and life
   To the weary, fainting soul.

All living things rejoice to feel
   Thy light wings floating nigh,
And hail thee with a welcome voice,
   As thou art passing by.

All nature wakes to life and song,
　Beneath thy light wings fanned,
Ye bear delight where'er ye roam,
　O'er all the world's fair land.

Light winds, light winds, pass onward,
　Light winds, pass gently by,
With thy cooling breeze and balmy breath,
　On, on through the boundless sky

Light winds, light winds, we praise the power,
　That gave thy fair winds birth,
That wafts thy balmy breath of life,
　O'er all the fainting earth.

ONE HUNDRED YEARS FROM NOW.

One hundred years from now the world may roll
Round on its orbit, steadily, from pole to pole;
The sun's bright orb still shine from realms afar,
And night bring forth the rays of glittering star;
But we'll have fled, the soul of man hath fled;
All mortal life, now living, lieth dead;
Silent and motionless beneath the withering sod,
Awaiting resurrection and the summons of our
   God.

One hundred years from now, ah, then
How little will be reck'ed of us by men
In the busy world, still moving on apace,
E'en the faintest shadows of ourselves can trace;
Then 'mong the many living who shall care,
Whether we come, or go, or whence, or where,
Our passing sorrows, griefs and joy, or pain,
Our longings, strivings, strugglings for gain.

All are forgotten in these newer walks of life,
Our vain ambitions, aspirations, strife,
Our seeking for the plaudings of friends, and fame,

Our praise, our condemnation, worthiness or
    blame,
All vanished with the rue, or laurel, on our brow;
Fading to oblivion one hundred years from now,
All, save our good or evil influence, ever rife,
Shaping each human destiny, each future life.

OUR HEROES.

Peering down long ages of historic time,

There merges on the vision, in a marshaled line,

Each leader and each hero who hath won a name,

In the great world's annals of immortal fame;

They stand, a grand, invincible, unvanquished
band,

With victory's symbol held aloft in each con-
queror's hand.

Marching along the corridors of vanished time,

Come stately forms of heroes, from every far off
clime.

There stands an Alexander, with his brave warrior bands,

Pointing with exultation to his conquered lands;

And Cæsar's banners, floating where conquered
nations weep,

Point to a proud world bending in submission at
his feet.

Again the vision changes, and Napoleon, regal,
grand,

Comes, like a flashing meteor, by ambition's fires
fanned,

And wields the sword of conquest, proud heights
of power to gain,

Mounts the high pinnacles of glory, to victory
and fame.

March on, march on, ye heroes, with banners all
unfurled,

With bugles loudly sounding, ye conquerors of
the world.

March on, thou valiant heroes, from every nation,
 clime,
Swiftly do their forms recede adown the aisles of
 time.
Sound, sound aloud the trumpet! let banners o'er
 thee wave!
The laurels of brave victories won lie o'er each
 hero's grave.
Furl, furl the banners o'er them, o'er the heroes
 in their pride,
They lived and fought for conquest, and for glory
 they died.

* * * * * * *

Adown the aisles of vision, adown the marshaled
 line,
Columbia's heroes are advancing, keeping pace
 with time;
Slowly down the vista, glides a form of regal
 height,
God-like in strength and valor, God-like in strength
 and might.
Columbia's famed hero, proud, stately, in command,

Brave Washington, their leader, the father of
  our land.
Loudly the bugle's sounding, loudly the trumpets
  call,
They are marching on toward victory, our heroes,
  one and all;
For liberty and freedom, for liberty and right,
Gallantly our heroes struggle 'mid the thickest
  of the fight.
Charge on! charge on, ye heroes! ye leaders of
  the fray,
Charge on! charge on for freedom, whilst your
  people watch and pray.
Loudly the trumpet's sounding, loudly the can-
  nons roar,
Steadily they are pacing on, each leader to the
  fore;
With every eye uplifted and every poiniard bent,
They charge upon oppression, and Columbia's
  chains are rent.
Columbia forever! let the banners o'er thee wave,
"The land of the free and the home of the brave."

    *   *   *   *   *   *   *   *

Once again the signal's sounding, 'mid the can-
    non's deafening roar,
To arms! To arms! Our country's calling our
    heroes to the fore.
Darkly gleams the cloud oppression, spreading
    on from shore to shore,
Bowed beneath the yoke of slavery. See! Our
    nation weeps once more.
Solemnly the drums are beating. To arms! To
    arms! Again they call,
As our heroes, wounded, bleeding, shout for vic-
    tory as they fall.

High above the raging battle, where foes strug-
    gle hand to hand,
Plunging 'mid the fiercest conflict, brave Ulysses
    shouts in stern command,
"On for liberty and freedom, on for liberty and
    right!"
Hosts on hosts of heroes follow, charging in their
    strength and might.

Backward falls the vanquished tyrant, backward
falls our freedom's foe,
And the starry spangled banner waves in triumph
to and fro.

Hark! the bugle notes are pealing, floats our
standard high and free,
And our nation's loudly sounding their glad
shouts of victory.
Sound the trumpets, wave the banners, let the
booming cannon roar,
And our standard be for freedom, freedom now,
forever more.
Let the cry ring on forever, echo on o'er land
and sea,
Freedom for each man and nation—freedom and
sweet liberty.

       *   *   *   *   *   *   *   *

There were sounds of loud rejoicing, on that
victorious day,
When the darkening clouds of slavery were forever swept away;

High the bugle notes were sounding, echoed forth
the trumpet's blast,
In honor of our freeborn nation, and her struggle
o'er and past.

Brightly shone the sky above us, gleamed the
sunlight's golden ray,
O'er the starry spangled banners, as they waved
in triumph free;
Rolled the cannons' reverberations o'er the land
from sea to sea,
And our nation joyfully sounded her glad shouts
of victory.

Hark! amid the echoes rolling ever on from shore
to shore,
Solemnly the bells are tolling 'mid the cannons'
muffled roar,
And above our martyred chieftain weeps our
nation o'er his bier;
O'er our slain and martyred hero now is shed the
silent tear.

Solemnly the bells are tolling, furl the banners
o'er his breast;
Peacefully sleeps our martyred Lincoln, lay his
honored form to rest.

God-inspired in right and wisdom, God-inspired
in strength he came,
Lifted up our falling nation, saved it from a tar-
nished name;
Every heart is bowed in sorrow, every banner
closely furled,
O'er the form of our loved hero—every heart
with grief is stirred.

Honored of the world and nation, idol of our
hearts and pride,
Savior of our cause and country, brave and true
our hero died.
Grandly lies his form and stately, 'neath our cities'
pillared halls,
And sweet anthems, like the sea waves, solemnly
arise and fall.

Toll the bells, awake the echoes, o'er the land
    from sea to sea,
Our brave hero lies a martyr to our land and
    liberty.

Solemnly the dirge is chanted, folded the banners
    o'er his breast,
Peacefully our martyr's sleeping, forever lies his
    form at rest;
Every heart is bowed in sorrow, every heart is
    stilled with grief,
O'er the form of our loved chieftain bends our
    nation now to weep;
Solemnly the bells are tolling, tolling, tolling,
    o'er and o'er,
Fare thee well, our loved chieftain, fare thee well
    forever more.

O, Liberty! Thou, with freedom's sunlight streaming o'er thy brow,
Turn thy fair gaze upon each struggling nation
  now,
Banish the gathering shadows from freedom's
  waning light,
And flash thy glorious scepter of liberty and
  right.

Flash forth thy gleaming beauty, all radiant and
  bright,
And crush the rising tyrants down, beneath thy
  power and might;
Deep in the heart of nations, where corruption
  shadows creep,
Turn thy fair gaze e'en there, Fair Liberty, where
  justice lies asleep.

Send forth thy piercing lances, with a purifying
  gleam,
Arouse her quick'ning conscience, awake her
  from her dream;

Banish the misty shadows, fast gathering o'er
　thy way,
Hail! hail! Sweet Liberty! let freedom reign
　for aye!
Hail! hail! all hail, Fair Goddess! we clasp thee
　by the hand,
And crown thee with our blessings, thou ruler
　of our land.

THE SOLDIERS' SLEEP.

They sleep, our heroes, who fought and bled,
They sleep 'neath the sod with the mingled dead;
They sleep, and 'neath fall of the evening dew
We bend o'er their graves for a sad adieu.

They sleep, they sleep, we have laid them low.
Where the drooping shades wave to and fro.
They rest, where the tall tree branches wave
O'er their gallant forms, in their quiet grave.

They sleep, their spirit forms have fled;
We weep o'er their lonely moss-grown bed.
They sleep, their spirits have passed to rest,
To their home with the redeemed and blessed.

Farewell, farewell, to their lonely tomb;
They sleep 'neath the shades of the evening gloom.
Asleep, asleep, in their lonely bed,
Farewell, farewell, to our cherished dead.

They sleep, and victory's gained at last,
Their conflict o'er, and their struggles past.
They rest, and our banners of freedom wave
O'er their gallant forms, in their honored grave.

HINCKLEY IN FLAMES.

Oh, had I the pen of the poet,
And the eloquent muse of old,
Then could I describe the terrors
Of the fiery fiends uncontrolled,
As they swept and danced through the forest,
Like billowy waves, onward rolled,
Leaped skyward, like demons exulting,
Striding on in their merciless tread,
Mocking at waste and ruins,
They left in their trail as they fled.
Homes, now deserted, in ashes,
With awe, doth the stranger pass by,
And listening he heareth strange echoes,
They come to him low, like a sigh.
The moans of the dead and dying,
The wail of the child by the way,
Who has fled in fright and terror,
Knowing scarce whither to stray,
Crouching to the ground in anguish,
Reaching arms upward to pray,
When, lo, the flames are upon them,
Consuming their young life away.

Aged parents flee onward together,
Their feeble steps palsied by pain,
Together they falter, they perish,
Pursued by the demon of flame.
Fiercer the flames are advancing,
And day seems turned into night,
There is rushing of feet in the forest,
And hundreds of souls take their flight.
On, on, and on they are rushing,
Some haven of refuge to gain;
Hail, joy, there is help in the distance,
Root, the hero, with fast flying train.
Sturdily brave and so dauntless,
Standing there in the glare of the flame,
Rescuing souls who are perishing,
Regardless of praise or of blame,
Just doing his duty most manlike—
What hero need boast of more fame?
There's a shout of joy and thanksgiving,
Goes up from that struggling throng,
As they feel the wheels of God's chariot
Swiftly bearing them on.
On, on, o'er the hill and the valley,

On, on, o'er the field and plain,
Reaching a place of safety
Through seas of smoke and flame.
Yet, hark, e'en here in safe harbor,
What agonized sobs rend the air,
Poor, grief-stricken souls in abandon,
Seeking lost friends here and there.
Calling in vain to the dying,
Weeping in vain o'er the dead,
Till the stoutest hearts filled with compassion,
And weak souls turned and fled.
Hark! like a bugle is sounding
The call, which thrills through the land,
"Bring aid" to these sufferers, and quickly
Extend them a strong, helping hand.
Brave, generous hearts, ever ready,
Respond to their eager demand,
Giving aid to hearts which are sinking,
Giving hope to souls in despair;
Thus nobly are people responding,
Hearing and answering their prayer.
Draw softly the veil o'er the picture
No human tongue can describe,
But leave to recording angels
That which to man is denied.

A LEAP TO DEATH OF CHICAGO FIREMEN.

AT THE WORLD'S FAIR.

Hurled to eternity, down, down to death,
Down through the seething flames' fiery breath,
Where are the hardened hearts bearing the blame?
Hurled to eternity, down through the flame,
Recklessly, helplessly, brave men are slain.

Mount, mount your buildings, reared to the sky,
Ordering brave men up, to perish and die;
Hurled to eternity, down, down to death,
Down through the seething flames' fiery breath,
Hurled to eternity, down to their death.

Heeding no warning, the order was given,
Up, up and upward brave men were driven;
Recklessly, helplessly, sent to their doom,
For aid calling loudly, but pleading in vain,
Recklessly, helplessly, brave men were slain.

Oh, world of humanity, mighty and strong,

How long must selfish injustice be borne?

Hopelessly, helplessly, the brave still are doomed;

For aid they are calling, must their pleadings be
  vain?

Recklessly, helplessly, brave men are slain.

SACRED POEMS.

OVER THE RIVER.

Oh, beautiful land, where storms never come,
Where the summer of sunlight is streaming,
Earth clouds and tempests forever are done,
And the sun in its beauty is gleaming.
    Over the river, over the river,
      We'll seek that beautiful home.

Oh, beautiful land, where clouds ne'er stray,
Where the summer of sunlight ne'er fades away,
We list to the songs of the white-winged bands,
Afloat through the vales of the summer land,
    As they welcome our spirits home,
      Welcome our spirits home.

Sweet sounds of music roll over the plain,
And seraphims join in the glad refrain,
Oh, come to the land where all is bright,
Where gleams the rays of eternal light,
　　Oh, come thou wanderer, come,
　　　Come, thou wanderer, come.

Oh, land with thy beautiful gates ajar,
We are passing on and o'er the bar,
Over life's seething and restless tide,
Over the river we soon shall glide,
　　Oh, bear our spirits home,
　　　Bear our spirits home.

Over the river, we soon shall hear
The dip of the oar, as they're gliding near,
Over the river, the beck'ning band
Will welcome us home to the summer land,
　　Welcome our spirits home,
　　　Welcome our spirits home.

A REQUIEM.

Hush, hush, ye mortal throng, thy weeping,
  Sorrowing o'er the shrouded bier;
Hush, hush, the weary soul is sleeping,
  Seraph forms are hovering near.

Thou'st past through the billows of the deep,
  Rest, rest, rest, rest and sleep,
  Rest, rest, rest, rest and sleep.

Bow low while seraph forms are voicing
  Their dirges, low and sweet;
Wake not again to mortal weeping,
  Rest, rest, rest, rest and sleep.

Peace, peace to thy silent form there sleeping,
  Peace, peace be to thy soul,
Soon wilt thou wake to heavenly greeting,
  To life and bliss untold.

EASTER DAWN.

Lo, the dawn of light is breaking,
O'er the hilltops far away;
Hark, glad notes of triumph sounding,
Christ our Lord has risen to-day.

Holy angels sweetly chanting,
Christ our Lord has risen to-day;
Earthly voices joyfully blending,
Borne on wings of light away.

Holy, holy angel voices
Chants aloud our glad refrain,
Glory to God in the highest, glory,
Glory to God, amen, amen.

CHORUS.

At the pearly bars of heaven,
Sound aloud the glad refrain,
Glory in the highest, glory,
Amen, amen, amen.

170

EASTER DAWN.

Lo, the dawn of light is breaking,
O'er the hilltops far away.

WAITING.

Waiting and watching at evening,
For the great, bright lights to appear,
Along the dark banks of the horizon
Of our shadowy journey here.

Waiting, watching, longing,
With joy unspeakable, too,
As we catch the gleam of radiance,
As the lights come drifting through.

Waiting for the clouds of darkness
In the night to roll away,
Waiting the glorious summons
That shall herald the brighter day.

Waiting the beautiful haven,
That glorious place of rest,
Waiting a message from heaven
To join the ransomed and blest.

Waiting, watching, hoping,
Till the journey of life is passed,
Waiting to gain the harbor
Of eternal rest at last.

WHAT IS DEATH?

What is death?   It is the breaking
Of the spirit's bondage here,
And to blissful life awaking,
Free from grief and fear.

'Tis the laying down of sorrow,
At the weary close of day,
And arising on the morrow,
Never more to know decay.

What is Death?   It is the dawning
Of the soul's immortal light,
Where the joyous beams of morning
Sweep away the clouds of night.

'Tis the spirit's blest reunion
With the loved ones gone before,
Where our souls shall hold communion
With the loved ones evermore.

What is Death?   Oh, spirit weary,
On the Rock of Ages cast,
Lo, the angels hovering near thee,
Is a guide to heavenly rest.

Let no trembling thoughts oppress thee,
Trust in the Redeemer's love,
Smilingly he waits to greet thee,
'Mid the heavenly courts above.

CHRISTMAS TIME.

All hail, all hail, this happy Christmas morn,
Christ, the infant child, to earth is born,
The holy harbinger of glad tidings from afar,
Hail, hail our Christ, our Lord, our guiding star.

Hail, hail, oh, yearning hearts in need,
Christ hath bid our captive souls be freed;
Hail, hail, this holy Christmas morn,
Christ, our Lord, our King, is born.

Hail, hail, all hail, let joyous voices ring,
In praise to Christ, our Lord, Immanuel, King;
Let joyous bells ring out a merry Christmas cheer,
Hail, hail the happiest, gladdest day of all the
year.

AFTER THE NIGHT.

Must Life's path be ever shrouded,
'Mid night shades' deep'ning gloom?
Must we seek and pray forever,
For one ray of springtime's bloom?
Must all the clouds and shadows
Be borne along our way,
And all glad light and sunbeams
From our pathway stray?
Must Life's path lead through deserts,
By the wild woods' thorny way,
And Life's glad happiness and joy
'Mid night shades fade away?

Hark, through the lone wilderness
Comes a sweet sound, soft and clear,
Like a trumpet, it is sounding,
O'er the hilltops far and near:
"I am thy Lord, thy shepherd,
Thou pilgrim have no fear,"
By still waters and through valleys,
And 'mid edens of delight,
Shalt thy freed soul journey onward,
After the night.

After the night
Comes realms of endless day,
After the night
The shadows of earth shall fade away,
And thy ransomed soul with ecstacy replete,
Shalt bow with adoration
At thy Savior's feet;
For out of darkness into endless light
Shalt thy freed soul journey onward,
After the night.

DYING.

Passing beyond life's vision,
Passing out of sight,
Stepping out of darkness
Into realms of light.

Passing beyond life's shadows,
Passing beyond the bar,
Passing through the Pearly Gates,
Which were left ajar.

Passing from earth to Heaven
Into eternal rest,
Joining our loved and lost ones,
Joining the loved and blest.

Why do we call it dying?
Life is but a breath.
Why do we call it dying?
Why do we call it death?

*   *   *   *   *

"Passing out of the shadow
Into a purer light;
Stepping behind the curtain
Getting a clearer sight.

Laying aside the burden,
This weary mortal coil;
Done with the world's vexations,
Done with its tears and toil.

Tired of all earth's playthings,
Heartsick and ready to sleep,
Ready to bid our friends farewell,
Wondering why they weep.

Passing out of the shadow,
Into eternal day.
Why do we call it dying,
This sweet going away?"

OUR CROSS TO BEAR.

Savior, ours the cross to bear alway,
And each and every hour will pray,
In joy or sorrow,
Or, when weary and oppressed,
And needing rest,
Thou would'st suffer us
To lean hard against thy breast,
There finding comfort.

Knowing we are blessed
With Thy strength and power,
To follow in Thy footstep
Hour by hour;
To follow in the footsteps
Thou hast trod,
Which leads ever to Thee,
And Heaven and God.

IS THE SPIRIT IMMORTAL?

Is the spirit immortal where thou art?
Is there perfect redemption of soul?
Doth the spirit, when redeemed from its sinning,
Reach a higher, a happier goal?

Doth the soul in its purified beauty,
From the mansions in heaven above,
Stoop earthward, in boundless longing,
And shield us and guide us with love?

Do our souls hear thy soft, gliding footsteps?
Do we hear thy soft, whispered tone?
Doth thy sweet influence surround us
When our thoughts dwell on thee when alone?

From the eternal spheres of hereafter
Comes there no message to me?
Yes, wafted from spheres supernal
Comes this innermost answer from thee.

As long as the soul in its bondage
Doth struggle from sin to be free,
Doth the heaven-sent angels stoop earthward
As ministering spirits to thee.

IN THE HUSH OF NIGHT.

Oft in the hush of night,
'Mid God's own holy light,
When the bright angels seem
Through space to shine and gleam,
When the fair moon of night
    Sheds her pale beam.

Oft in the still, lone hour,
Touched by an unseen power,
Comes then this thought to me,
    Over life's restless sea:
Oh, that my life might shine
With God's sweet love divine,
When death with beckoning hand,
Points to that far off land,
    Points to my doom,
Points through the silent void,
    Points through the gloom.

When my last work is done,
When my last song is sung,
    When by the way I fall,
Answering the Master's call,
Then will my harvest gleaned
    Be great, or small.

JOURNEYING HOME.

We're journeying to our distant home,
  To that country far away,
Treading the path Christ hath trod,
  With Him to lead the way.

Drifting through deep, dark waters,
  On o'er the billowy tide,
We're journeying to our heavenly home,
  With Him for our dear guide.

On, on we're journeying, ever on,
  Through darkness of the night,
With His own hand to lead the way,
  And guide our steps aright.

Journeying beyond the shadowy tide
  Of life's rough, restless crest,
Journeying on to our heavenly home,
  Fair Eden—land of rest.

DAY BY DAY.

Day by day God's hand doth guard us,
   O'er life's calm or troubled sea,
What, though clouds and storms enshroud us,
   Hark, He whispers, "Trust in Me."

Day by day God sheds his radiance,
   Makes our duties plain to see,
What though thy task be rude and grievous,
   Hark, He whispers, "Lean on Me."

Day by day God scatters blessings
   O'er his children full and free,
Though thy needs be sore and pressing,
   Hark, He whispers, "Look to Me."

Day by day he soothes and strengthens,
   When we to his footstool flee,
Though we suffer pain and anguish,
   Hark, He whispers, "Come to Me."

COME UNTO ME.

Precious promise God hath given,
To the weary and oppressed,
Come unto Me, and coming,
I will give thee rest.

Rest from the weary cares of life,
Rest from misery, pain and strife,
Rest for our souls by waters sweet,
Rest for the weary pilgrim's feet.

Precious promise God hath given,
To the weary, sin-sick soul,
Come unto Me, and coming,
I will make thee whole.

Will cleanse thy sinful, guilty heart,
Will cause repentant tears to start,
Will shield thee with a mighty love,
Will guide thee to thy home above.

And when that awful hour hath come,
And we lay us down to die,
This precious promise still is given,
Fear not, for I am nigh.

Yes, near, to soothe our souls to rest,
Yes, near to fold us to His breast,
Yes, near, oh, happiness untold,
Yes, near, to guide us to His fold.

Oh, Savior, now we render thanks
For this precious promise given,
For Thy love and guidance here on earth,
And eternal rest in heaven.

EARTHLY HOPES.

Earthly hopes we know are fading,
  Earthly pleasures soon are past,
In heavenly joy forever vernal,
  We shall find sweet rest at last.

Earthly hopes, oh, how we struggle,
  How we reach and grasp,
But they, like a phantom,
  Soon elude us and are passed.

Earthly hopes are but the shadows
  Of our heavenly joys divine,
Of our hopes of life eternal,
  Where there's love and peace sublime.

Oh, there is a better clime,
  Where the Savior's light doth shine,
Where no wintry, chilling blast
  Can wreck our earthly hopes at last.

IF I COULD CHANGE.

If I could change, or could be born again,
I would be strong, I would be free from pain;
Take up my life, begin anew again.
I would be endowed with virtue, pure, refined;
I would show the inborn beauty of the mind;
I would be gifted with intellect sublime,
I would be master of both prose and rhyme.
I would be endowed with language to thrill
The human heart with noblest sentiments at will.
I would be gifted with power to inspire,
And grant to every heart its purest desire;
Would guide a struggling brother to a higher aim;
Would have the power to shield from wrong, the
    weak from blame.
I would have a soul, though inclosed in rudest
    clay,
I would, like the modeling artist, mould defects
    away;
I would chisel every blemish from the statue I
    should rear;
I would be my own ideal, like marble white and
    clear.

I would seek the weak and helpless, bid each
    fallen soul to mount,
Would bid each thirsty soul to seek pure waters
    at God's fount;
I would have the Christ-like power, divinely from
    above,
To weld the earthly universe in a brotherhood of
    love.

A SOLILOQUY ON DEATH.

Soon, soon I'll hear the solemn stroke
Of death's dread hour,
When from my nerveless hands will fall
Life's magic power;
And gazing out and o'er the lovely earth,
There comes to me the sound of joy and mirth,
The glad, gay laughter of the happy child,
Who looks into my sad, dim eyes and smiles.
Oh, earth, and home, and friends,
And all of this earth so fair and bright,
Farewell, farewell, to thee, and all,
Good night, good night.

The silvery moon shines brightly from afar,
And through the realms of space
There gleams the shining star.
Oh, earth, sweet earth, bathed in liquid light,
Thou art drifting, drifting from my sight.
Now comes the solemn stroke
Of death's signal bell,
Oh, earth, and home, and friends and all
Farewell, farewell.

DESPAIR AND HOPE.

See, the clouds of despair are settling,
Lowering fiercely, darkly o'er;
List the sullen roar of the winds,
And the breakers on the shore.

Onward, onward, fiercer grows the storm,
Hear the winds shriek and wail;
Onward, onward, the soul is borne;
Away, away, on the maddening gale.

On come the billows, higher, higher,
Drowning each hope and each desire,
See him quiver and shake in the blast.
Despair has reached his soul at last.

Despair, despair, so deep and dark,
Despair, what more is in his heart?
Death and self-murder o'ershadow him now;
Ah, yes, 'tis stamped upon his brow.

Hear the winds shrieking, sobbing, moaning,
Hear the poor soul in bitterness groaning,
Hear the winds shriek, hear them rave,
He is on the brink of a murderer's grave.

Whilst near him stood a form of light,
An angel clad in robes of white.

Despair has reached his soul at last,
The conflict o'er, the storm is past;
Despair, despair, he moaning cries,
Despair, despair, the wind replies.

And raising aloft his blood-shot eyes,
Almighty God, the poor soul cries—
Another shudder, another sigh,
Almighty God, forgive, I die.

As he raised his arm for the fearful stroke,
A sudden vision o'er him broke,
Staying his arm with its magic spell—
Saved, saved, he murmured, and fell.

Fell on his knees, with streaming eyes,
And with awe and rapture gazed;
Out of the darkness a star of hope
Steadily and brightly blazed.

Whilst near him stood a form of light,
An angel clad in robes of white,
Pointing to the glittering star,
That shone in the distance still afar.

See, the clouds of despair are breaking,
Vanishing far in the night;
See, a silvery veil unfolding,
Betokening dawn of light.

Brighter, brighter, grows the veil,
With a rosy tinted hue;
Brighter, brighter, the star appears,
And sheds its radiance through.

Thus the beautiful vision fades,
Fades away in the night,
But the star of hope still lingers
To guide his steps aright.

REMORSE.

Ah, yes, these memories, with what subtle power
Can'st bow the sinner's head, in a stilly hour,
Causing his heart to start and shrink with dread,
As at approach of shrouded ghost, or phantom's
    tread.

Memories of some foul deed, at dead of night,
Crowd in upon him, till pale with fright
He shrinks appalled, as memory's cruel grasp
Calls up the fearful recollections of the past

Memories of some foul deed or deadly crime
Spring up afresh, to haunt his guilty mind,
Whilst shadowy spectres seem to rise,
And transfix him with their gleaming eyes.

Again he sees the weapon's cruel gleam,
Hears his victim's piercing scream,
Or sees a dead, white, upturned face,
Locked in death's cold, still embrace.

Away, away, he moans, he shrieks,
As ashy grows his ghastly cheeks,

Still memory holds him in bondage fast,
Till his craven heart grows mad at last.

Mad, mad, mad, shrieking for aid,
He sinks at last in a murderer's grave.
All unforgiven his soul takes flight,
Out in the darkness of the night.

A SOLILOQUY.

The world, the world, we scorn
Its deceit and vanity;
   Humanity, humanity,
Had we more faith in thee.

The world, the world, what cares
   The world
If one more heart is wounded,
   Has bled?
What cares the world if one more heart
   Lies, like ashes, cold
     And dead?

CALUMNY.

How like a poisonous serpent,
Doth thou rear thy loathsome head.
Oh, Calumny, and with thy forked
Tongue of rankest venom, seek
With foulsome blow and well
Directed aim to fell thy victim.
Innocent although he be, thou'st
Smirch, with foul pollution, a fair
Good name,   Oh, slanderous soul,
Beset about by thine own rank
And hideous nature, fain would
The innocent, in pity rife for thee,
Forget their wounds, in wondering
Contemplation of so base, so vile
A thing, ensconced within the
Baleful soul that man calls human.

CAPTIVITY.

As the captive bird strikes its helpless wing
'Gainst the prison bar that shut it in,
Gazing the while with watchful, eager eye,
As his gay plumed comrades flutter by,
Unmindful of his pleading, plaintive cry,
Whirl on and upward through the sunlit sky,
Nor backward turn, ne'er stop or wait,
But leave their doomed companion to unhappy
    fate.

Thus many captive souls gaze wistfully, in vain,
For the breaking of their bonds, their captive
    chain;
Peering longingly through dungeon's prison bar
For one ray of hope, e'en one faint gleaming star,
To burst their bonds and set their gates ajar.
Thus struggling for freedom, their wanton fate
Glides calmly on: though eagerly the captives
    wait,
Fate turns not again to ope their prison gate.

YOUTH.

In youth, in thy life's early morning,
In the bloom of life's early spring,
Keep thy heart pure, white unsullied,
Let no serpent of evil creep in.

Press onward, and ever press upward,
Let no false lights lead thee astray;
And God, in his love and mercy,
Will lead thee and show thee the way.

Let thy thoughts be ever pursuing
The highest and noblest aim,
So that purpose and action combining,
Will win thee a crown of fame.

Will win thee a crown everlasting,
No earthly renown can gain;
Will win thee a crown eternal,
Where joy and happiness reign.

JUVENILE POEMS.

JUVENILE POEMS.

TO-NIGHT WHEN I PRAY.

I love you, I love you, please bend down your
head,
I want to kiss ma-ma, my little one said,
I saved you that kiss, but I've been naughty to-
day,
I'll ask God to forgive me, to-night when I pray.

Whisperingly, pleadingly, with small arms up-
raised,
Into my bending face two tearful eyes gazed,
Good night, good night, still the faltering lips
say,
I'll ask God to forgive me, to-night when I pray.

Comforting words to a sad mother's heart,

When her dear ones seem drifting away in the

    dark,

Whisperingly, pleadingly, hear the sinful one say,

I'll ask God to forgive me, to-night when I pray.

GLEE SONG FOR CHILDREN.
Chorus Bird Whistles.

LISTEN TO THE BIRDIES SING.

GLEE SONG FOR CHILDREN.

Listen to the birdies sing,
Listen to their echoes ring,
  Down, down the valley,
Through, through the glen,
  Merrily, cheerily,
Spring has come again.

Listen to their warbling notes,
As on the air they softly float,
  Down, down the valley,
Through, through the vale,
  Merrily, cheerily,
Through the flowery dale.

CHORUS.

Troll-la-la-troll-la-la,
Their gay songs echo near and far,
  Down, down the valley,
Through, through the glen,
  Merrily, cheerily,
Spring has come again.

Flitting skyward on the wing,
Listen to the birdies sing,
  Down, down the valley;
Up, up they soar,
  Merrily, cheerily,
Spring has come once more.

BRIGHT EYES.

Two little bright eyes, sparkling with fun,
Two little feet, tripping off on a run,
Two mirthful lips, smiling with glee,
We love you, we love you, our darling Louie.

Mamma, dear mamma, hear the sweet call,
Now up near the roof-top, now down in the hall,
Like the will-o-the-wisp, now here, and now there,
Flits our dear fairy, so sweet and so fair.

So like the song-birds, that sing in the spring,
And flutter and flit away on the wing,
Hear the sweet voice of our frolicsome fay,
Laughing and singing all the long day.

Gathering sweet flowers, the brightest that blow,
Hunting sweet clovers, the whitest that grow,
Oh, she's dear to our hearts, as dear as can be,
Our loving, our winsome, our darling Louie

BABY SONG.

Rocking, rocking, to and fro,
Away, away, away we'll go,
Where moonbeams shed their silvery light,
We'll glide away in the starry night;
Far, far away, o'er the waves we'll ride,
In a fairy boat away we'll glide,
Rocking, rocking, to and fro,
Away, away, away we'll go.

We'll sail away o'er the silvery stream,
Where the waters shine like a fairy's dream,
We'll float away on the foaming tide,
With our little darling by our side,
Rocking, rocking, to and fro,
Away, away, away, we'll go.

Far beneath the shadowy stream,
We'll watch the shadows shine and gleam,
Where the moonbeams shed their silvery light,
We'll glide away in the starry night,
Rocking, rocking, to and fro,
Away, away, away we'll go.

THE FAIRY DELL

AND OTHER POEMS.

WRITTEN IN EARLY YOUTH AND CHILDHOOD.

THE FAIRY DELL.

They wandered slowly through the dell,
The artist and the village belle,
He gathered flowers here and there,
And gave them to his love so fair.
At length they paused and looked around,
They stood transfixed, as if spell-bound,
For nature's murmuring voice they hear,
Whispering, whispering, far and near.

The artist gazed in awe profound,
Gazed long on the beauty reigning 'round,
Then spoke, and his tones fell soft and clear,
On the listening heart of the maiden near.
List, doth thou not hear the mighty sound?
It makes my heart within me bound.
Doth it not make thy soul rejoice,
When list'ning to sweet nature's voice?

Beyond, the sky, serenely blue,
Below, the earth, so green in hue,
Behold the mossy covered rocks,
Still wet with heaven's descending dew;

214

They wandered slowly through the dell,
The artist and the village belle.

The daisy's blossom, gold and white,
The pinks, the lilies, the violets bright,
The bees go humming round and round,
They know that sweets in them are found.

Oh, see the merry, sparkling brook,
As it gurgles and ripples on its way,
As it bubbles and laughs in its mirth and glee,
And seems to say, I'm free, I'm free.
The merry birds in bush and tree,
Flutter and flit from bough to lea,
All singing a joyous, tuneful lay,
And the dell seems to echo the gay melody.

And standing by the dancing brook,
The elk, the fawn, the antelope partook,
Then with shy, mischievous look,
Leaped up the steep and rocky nook,
And on the brink turned, looked 'round,
Then off to the forest with a bound,
Away, away up the rocky steep,
See their shadowy forms retreat.

*   *   *   *   *   *   *   *

The sun in the west is sinking low,
The lovers still wander to and fro,
The birds now seek their sheltering nests,
And fold their wings for a long night's rest.

But heeding naught of the flight of time,
They're listening to their young hearts' rhyme,
That sings of naught but joy supreme,
They plight their love as in a dream.
Plight their love 'mid hanging bowers
Of vines abloom with fragrant flowers,
Vowing eternal constancy,
Until no longer time shall be.

Thus wrapped in hymen's witching dream,
They float adown love's magic stream,
Whilst o'er their souls a calm is stealing—
A calmness as though sleeping, dreaming.

Or is it the charm of the enchanted dell,
That o'er them throws a strange, sweet spell?
They know not whether they wake or dream,
So heavenly sweet doth all things seem.

Away, away up the rocky steep,
See their shadowy forms retreat.

Thus bound in strange and sweet repose,
A fragrant ether around them flows,
On the night winds are borne sweet sounds
Of soft, sweet music floating 'round.

The leafy shadows around them blow,
Waving, dancing to and fro,
And shimmering through the mystic dell,
Strange, pale lights o'er the green turf fell;
And glancing through they caught the gleam
Of a thousand fairies' shine and sheen,
All floating below, around, above,
Singing and chanting songs of love.

Singing in cadence soft and low,
Of love and passion of long ago,
Of love that was happily charmed and blessed,
Of love that was faithfully true till death,
Of love that was severed and broken in twain,
Of love that was bound and united again,
Of love that was old, of love that was new,
Of love that was e'en to eternity true.

Sweet notes all atremble, they fall, they rise,
The dell re-echoes in strange replies,

Then slowly they fade in the mystic air,
Leaving the lovers wondering there.
Half roused from their strange, enchanting dream,
They awoke at length beside the stream,
Where their wandering feet had let them stray,
Ere the sun had set, and it yet was day.

Oh, murmured the beautiful village belle,
This surely must be the enchanted dell,
Where the lovely fairies dance all night,
In the shimmer and sheen of the bright moonlight.
And, oh, 'tis said, in the mystic hours,
When lovers have strayed to their mystic bowers,
They'll bless their love with a happy spell,
If they plight their troth in their fairy dell.

Yes, this must be enchanted land,
They murmured, standing hand in hand;
List, doth thou not hear that sweet, low sound?
It is, it is, enchanted ground.

        *   *   *   *   *   *   *

But as they spoke, their heads sank low
The moon shone soft and bright,

And o'er them floated mist on mist,
Of greenish, dazzling light,
And out of the mist there slowly came
A beautiful fairy queen;
And fold on fold, her golden robe
Swept the turft of green.

Slowly she waved her wand on high,
And summoned the youthful lovers nigh,
Then sang in accents low and sweet,
As they bowed themselves low at her feet

FAIRY SONG.

Noble youth and maiden fair,
Hear my warning and beware.
Cheeks have paled and tears have started,
Lovers have quarreled and lovers have parted
What art thy wishes, oh, happy pair?
To-night, to-night I'll heed thy prayer.
Wouldst thou forever happy be?
Then kneel, oh, kneel, oh, kneel to me.

Slowly they sank on the turfted ground,
Whilst sweet, low music floated round;

The moon shone bright thro' the dazzling mist—
But the youth is speaking, listen, list.

Beautiful, beautiful Fairy Bright,
There's but one wish we crave to-night;
Oh, surely, surely, love is thy spell;
We've plighted our troth in thy beautiful dell,
And in earth below, or heaven above,
Is there aught more pure, more sweet than love?
Oh, happy forever we shall be,
If forever thou'lt bind our ecstacy.

Noble youth and maiden fair,
To-night, to-night, I'll heed thy prayer;
Happy forever thou shalt be,
The charms of love shall dwell with thee,
Where e'er thou be.

Summoning a train of fairy sprites,
All 'rayed in robes of shining white,
She bade them pluck from their bosoms fair,
The flowers that were blooming there;

Summoning a train of fairy sprites,
All 'rayed in robes of shining white.

Slowly they twined them in the hair
Of the silent lovers kneeling there,
Then weaved them in a bridal chain,
And wound them round the happy twain.

Whilst o'er the turf they come and go,
Swaying and dancing to and fro,
Singing so soft 'twere like a sigh.
These flowers will live, they cannot die,
Emblems of all the virtues rare,
Wear them and keep them where e'er thou are.
Sweet flowers charmed by our magic spell—
Shield them, wear them, guard them well.

Sweet, sang the queen of the fairies bright,
Are the charms I endow thee with to-night;
The charms of patience, hope and faith,
The charms of truth and virtue's grace,
And pure hearts, with fidelity,
Will render strong thy constancy,
      Unto Eternity.

Again the fairy waved her wand,
And summoned her beautiful fairy band.

Along the dell there burst a sight,
Fairies, all gleaming, gold and white,
Shimmering, floating, dancing along,
The dell re-echoed their music and song;
The fairy queen danced on the velvety turf,
And joined in their song, and joined in their
    mirth.

Good night, they sing as they fade away,
Two more lives we've blessed for aye,
Happy forever they shall be,
Happy for eternity.

FAREWELL.

Farewell, farewell, though another's thou be,
Farewell, though thy smiles can ne'er be for me,
Though others may welcome, and others caress
   thee,
Though others may claim, and others may bless
   thee,
Still, when thy mind from every care free,
Still give but these moments in kind thoughts
   of me.

Or, when fortune's barque o'er calm seas may
   waft thee,
Or, when gliding by moonlight o'er calm summer's sea,
Or, when bright glittering stars in radiance shine
   o'er thee,
Oh, then, 'tis then, oh, then, think of me.

Farewell, farewell, forever we part,
Yet may my image still dwell in your heart,
Still, in the gloaming, remember the time,
We roamed 'neath the elms and alleys of lime,
When the night birds warbled their happiest strain,
Or sailed by the shores of some bright wooded
   stream.

Then here is my hand, my fair one, good-bye,
But, oh, that with me thou too might fly,
But since fate has severed the sweet, tender tie,
Then farewell forever, and a gentle good-bye.

FRIENDSHIP.

Out from her stately home
She came to my cottage door,
Kind were her looks and words,
And they'll linger forever more.

I would have been her friend,
With a clasp of hand for my lifelong fee;
Though I were nothing to her,
Still she was the world to me.

Say, how will it be with our souls
When we meet in that better land?
What the mortal could never know,
Will the spirit yet understand?

And in some celestial form
Will our friendship repeated be,
And I be something to her,
While she brightens heaven for me?

WHERE THE LILIES BEND.

In earth below or heaven above,
Is there aught more pure, more sweet than love?
Or in magic friendship's tender tie?
Ask of the lilies drooping nigh.

Close clasped hands, eyes meeting,
Low, kind words, hearts beating;

In signs like these a deep meaning lies,
Friendship born of the very skies.
Must aught so perfect have an end?
Ask where the slender lilies bend.

Ask where the tall trees whisper low,
Ask of the rose the winds doth blow;
Ask where the lilies droop and bend,
Must aught so perfect have an end?

Farewell, the leaves doth murmur as they blow,
Farewell, the lilies sigh it, bending to and fro,
Farewell, farewell, e'en the winds reply,
There's naught more painful than good bye;
Yes, aught so perfect must surely end,
Alone the rose and lilies bend.

FATE.

Two souls were born, each in foreign land,
While sullen Fate stood by,
Marked each with unrelenting hand;
Both were endowed with longings, aspirations
high,
Ne'er to be attained on earth,
Nor yet, until they die.

Both endowed with beauty, youth and grace,
Both endowed with pure souls, and chaste.
And one with honored, noble name,
And one with something akin to fame;
Still Fate stood mocking, gloating, nigh,
There's still some things she would these souls
deny.

'Tis knowing the anguish of the heart,
When at last they meet and love and part,
'Tis when eye meets eye, hand meets hand, soul
meets soul;
'Tis then Fate holds them in fierce control,
And mocks them, as struggling to the last,
She binds them in cruel fetters.

And fettered thus they grieve their lives away,

Longing, ever longing, for some other day,

Some other clime, where their two souls

Shall be united for an eternity of time,

And glide, like some calm stream,

Where life will ne'er prove to them a myth, a
    dream.

The following verses were written on reading a story, where the lover
is drowned at sea and the heroine goes insane, and spends her life wandering on the beach in search for him.

WHISPERING WINDS.

The winds are whispering to me, dear love,

Whispering and whispering to me,

It has wandered o'er summer sea, dear love,

And o'er hill and lea.

And now the winds are moaning, dear love

'Tis thy spirit sighing for me,

I see thou art beckoning to me, dear love,

As thy form glides over the sea.

As it glides o'er the sunlit isles, dear love,
And o'er the moonlit tide.
And soon, and soon I'll go, dear love,
And soon I'll be thy bride.

Thou art watching and waiting for me, dear love,
And I'll watch and wait for thee.
And soon, and soon, I'll come, dear love,
And soon I'll come to thee.

Side by side we'll wander, dear love,
And we'll glide o'er the glad sea foam,
But the winds are dying away, dear love,
Yet forever and ever we'll roam.

SEVERED.

Oh, I know that we are severed
  By a gulf we ne'er can span,
Until we meet in the golden streets
  Of a better, better land.

And, oh, my heart is heavy,
  Heavy with unshed tears,
Watching, waiting, longing,
  Till thy sweet soul reappears.

Till I see thy seraph form advance,
  Just without the golden portal,
Surrounded by sweet angel forms,
  All radiant and immortal.

Till I hear thy sweet voice calling
  To my struggling soul without;
Till the heavenly bars are opened wide,
  And we meet no more to part.

Oh, I know that we are severed
  By a gulf we ne'er can span,
But soon we'll meet in the golden streets
  Of a better, better land.

THE ORPHAN'S LAMENT.

Mother, mother, hear the whisper
Of my soul to thine,
Telling of the secret sadness,
Dwelling within my breast;
Telling of the pain and sadness,
And my soul's unrest.

Oh, for thy gentle hand's caress,
Oh, for thy gentle voice to bless,
Oh, for the magic of thy love,
To soothe my soul's unrest.

Mother, mother, can'st thou not hear
My anguished call to thee?
Only the echo of my calling
Answers back to me.
Gone, gone, thy spirit forever fled;
They laid thy saintly form from sight,
And said that thou wast dead.

Dead, dead, thy spirit fled,
Tell not this tale to me;
Oh, tell me not that love like thine,
Can perish eternally.

Mother, mother, I'll not believe
Thou art forever fled,
Yet, oh, the void within my heart,
And, oh, the weary pain.
And, oh, the weary, watching, longing,
Ere we shall meet again.

Yet, I have felt a strange delight,
I've felt thy spirit near to-night,
And thou hast whispered peace to me,
Until our souls united be.

Written when a child, after reading a book entitled Bethlehem's Star, sent by a Sabbath school teacher, when upon her death bed, as a token of love and last remembrance.

BETHLEHEM'S STAR.

Beloved friend in heaven,

What a token of thy love,

Hast left a youthful pilgrim,

Seeking her home above.

As I look upon these pages,

Oh, the pleasure that is mine,

Oh, the calmness that steals o'er me,

As I read each beauteous line,

Telling of the great Messiah,

And his wondrous love,

Beckoning us onward, onward,

To our home above.

Ah, yes, 'tis a greater treasure,

Than the gift of rarest kind,

To have impressed upon the mind,

God's great love divine.

A few words of God's holy love

239

Oft' times bring relief
To a soul that's wandering
In darkness, sin or grief.
Telling us that from afar
Still shines o'er us Bethlehem's Star.
Look to heaven, oh, youthful pilgrim,
Ere thou'st crossed life's desert plain,
Thou canst see the Star of Bethlehem
Brightly o'er thy pathway stream.

SONG.

Oh, here is a hand for our fellow man,
A hand for a friend or foe,
What e'er betide, the world is wide,
And smoothly onward we will glide,
Or if roughly tossed by the heaving tide,
 We'll paddle our own canoe,
  Paddle our own canoe.

Bounding along o'er the billowy foam,
We'll sing like boatmen true,
What e'er betide, the world is wide,
O'er calm blue seas or roughest tide,
We'll bend to the oar and onward ride;
 We'll paddle our own canoe,
  Paddle our own canoe.

Then here's a hand for our fellow man,
A hand for friend or foe,
Though foes be strong, or friends be few,
Of each and all we ne'er would sue;
 We'll paddle our own canoe,
  Paddle our own canoe.

SAILOR SONG.

We're sailors bold, of the wide, blue sea,
    We're sailors wild and free,
We sail our ships o'er the wide, wide sea;
    Oh, a sailor's life for me,
    A sailor's life for me.

Oh, ho, my boys, come sing with me,
    As our barque rides o'er the sea,
Come, let your voices ring loud, ring long,
    Hurrah, hurrah, we're free,
    We're sailors wild and free.

CHORUS.

Come, come, my boys, let's quaff the breeze,
    That makes us strong and free,
Oh, let the dear, old wild winds blow,
    As we sail away o'er the sea.
    As we sail away o'er the sea.

Up, up, my boys, there's a storm in view,
    Let our barque rush o'er the sea,
She'll stem the waves, she'll ride the tide,
    We're sailors bold and free,
    Sailors bold and free.

Oh, see the moon shines in the sky so high,
   And gleams o'er the waters deep,
And our staunch ship rides o'er the heaving tide,
   Where the foaming billows leap,
   Foaming billows leap.

We're sailors bold, of the wide, blue sea,
   My gallant crew and me,
Then hail to every one we meet,
   That sail their ships o'er the deep,
   That sail their ships o'er the deep.